A Ruined Life

By Skinphil

Forced to become an Aryan Brother

A Ruined Life

Skinphil

Copyright © 2014 Gay Books Fetish

Published at Amazon/Kindle through Gay Books Fetish

All rights reserved. No part of this book may be reproduced or transmitted in any form or by any means, electronic or mechanical, including photocopying, recording, or by any information storage and retrieval system, without permission in writing from the copyright owner. This book always remains the intellectual property of the writer under the Copyright Laws in Australia and the world.

This is a work of fiction. Names, characters, places and incidents either are the product of the author's imagination or are used fictitiously, and any resemblance to any persons, living or dead, events, or locales is entirely coincidental. Pictures used in this book are taken from the World Wide Web and are considered public property, and used only to portray a look. If you recognise any of these pictures as your property I apologise.

Should you wish to contact the author, please contact on this email address only.

Gaybooksfetish@gmail.com

Copyright © 2014 skinphil

All rights reserved.

ISBN-13: 978-1500962487

ISBN-10: 1500962481

Author's Note

Fictional stories are written to entertain so some aspects of a story may not be exactly what would be expected or known to be factual. Prisons are not the same in all respects but similar with discipline and rules. I have researched as much as I can to produce this story but I have also taken the liberty of trying to make it a story as well. Some will read this and think it incorrect in some aspects and rubbish the content, and to them I say thank you for at least reading it. If they want to contact me and express their concerns, they are welcome and maybe I can correct the issue in a later revision. A contact email address is shown under the copyright.

Prison life is hard, we all know that. The concept of this story is of prisons and how seemingly ordinary people can place their future in jeopardy through a stupid act and end up in a world far removed from what they consider their norm. This story is about a young man in the prime of his youth who acts stupidly and will pay for his stupidity for the rest of his life. We are all guilty of that at times. We all have choices in life and our decisions on those choices are what make our lives what they are. How often have you said "If only"? This story is about one man's decision: How he ruined his Life and ended up in prison for 20 years non-parole period. But was he really to blame?

Phil Lesbirel

Preface

How often have you finished work or just met friends on the weekend for drinks and maybe a nightclub or party afterwards. We all do it and never think of the consequences of how we will get home afterwards should we drink to excess. Malcombe Everett was a typical youth of 18 years old; brash, eager to fit in, wanting a good life at the end of his University studies; a family and the usual house with the white picket fence. He had just passed his driving test and his father had bought him a 1992 Buick LeSabre and although it looked good, it was telling its age with the interior worn but still decent transport for a young man. Malcombe loved his car and was the envy of his friends who; as yet; were still using dads car or on public transport. Having finished college in December of 2001, Malcombe was looking forward to entering UCLA in February of 2002 to study Law. His father was a prominent Commercial Lawyer and had promised him a position in the firm on his graduation.

It was a few days before Christmas 2001 and he was meeting friends for drinks before the holiday season. It was at a bar in the centre of Los Angeles and they were going on to a night club afterwards. Malcombe promised to drive everyone home. They all had a few drinks; ales or spirits as they preferred; then Malcombe drove them down town to the night club district. He found a car parking space quickly then they all walked around the area until they found a nightclub to their liking. They partied until well after 3 am before deciding to call it a night. Malcombe did not consider himself drunk by any means and quite happily sat in the driver's seat, his girl friend Rebecca next to him. His friend Alex Bosset sat on the outside of the front seat, Mandy Draper sat with her boy friend Heinrick Berger in the back and Alex's girlfriend Peta Graves sat directly behind Alex and was cuddling his head and shoulders, leaning forward. Then Malcombe collapsed.

Chapter 1

I was confused when I opened my eyes. I hurt in every part of my body; huge pains down my left side; my shoulders, face, legs and torso. I couldn't open my eyes as they were all stuck together. Someone was calling my name and when I tried to answer all that came out was a cough and a guttural sound.

"It's ok Malcombe, just relax while we clean you up and maybe then you can see and talk." I had no idea who was talking but the voice was soothing. The pain was excruciating and I wanted it to go away. I felt hands exploring my legs and I heard a voice; male voice; say that it was broken but he wanted a full scan of the body and head. The female voice agreed and said she would clean me up first then send me down for a CTI. When she cleaned up my eyes and sucked out my throat, I could see I was in hospital but I couldn't move my head or body as I was strapped down. My eyes worked although it was hard to see as they were swollen. My throat hurt badly from the suction tube as well as from an injury and I could not breathe through my nose. I could see the female voice was a middle aged nurse, and she then inserted the suction tube into my nose and I found I could breathe a little better but not much.

"We will have to fix that for you so you can breathe better. Your nose is broken and rather flat at the moment. We are sending you down to X-ray for a CTI scan as we think you may have internal as well as head injuries. You definitely have a broken leg in 2 places as well as your collar bone and right arm. I was wheeled down to X-ray and into a room with a CTI scanning machine. I was lifted gently onto the machine, but I tried to scream out in pain but just a loud sound emanated from the throat. But the pain subsided and

I was lying on the CTI bed. The Radiologist then told me to relax and the bed then started to move. First my head then it moved down slowly until it had covered the whole of my body. Finished, I was then taken back to where I had come from and I assumed it was the emergency section of the hospital. The thought came to me: If I was injured, were any of my friends in the car with me injured? What had happened? The results were in and the doctor came in to see me.

"Malcombe, you are a lucky man. No serious head injuries so that will heal quickly. The collar bone is broken so a few weeks in plaster there, 3 cracked ribs, but what worries me most is the bruising and bleeding of the liver. It should recover but you might find blood in your urine for a few weeks. Your left leg is broken and so is your left ankle. From what I was told briefly by the police, you were lucky to have survived the crash."

"What happened to my friends in the car doctor?"

"I'm sorry I can't tell you that. You will have to ask the police when they interview you later."

I went from section to section as they plastered up my leg and collar bone; strapped my ribs and cleaned and bandaged my head. It took hours to complete and was very painful. When all was done, I was taken to a ward; but not a normal ward: It was a prison ward. I didn't know what was happening as they cuffed my right arm to the bed then locked the door behind them as they left. I was alone now and in great pain but confused about the room I was in. but that was answered after about 2 hours. Two men walked into the room and asked my name. I was then read my rights and then charged with 5 counts of Culpable Homicide. My head was reeling now and the questions I had would not come out. Then I found my voice.

"What happened? Will someone tell me what happened? Are my friends ok?" I was not thinking and did not link the 5 charges of culpable homicide to their deaths. "Can you please tell me what happened; please?"

"You were driving whilst intoxicated and lost control of the car, slamming into a power pole then cutting across the freeway and head on into a truck. The car was cut in half and your passengers thrown out onto the roadway. You were the only passenger who remained in the car thus you sustained serious injuries but were still alive when police and ambulance arrived. Your passengers were all dead at the scene. You will be transferred to a prison hospital tomorrow to await a preliminary hearing. I wouldn't be thinking about freedom for a while lad." They then walked out with the door being locked once again.

Charged with 5 counts of culpable homicide? I knew from reading the paper and from the TV that culpable homicide was 20 years to life and 5 counts was my entire life and more. I would die in prison. How could I have been so drunk and so stupid to have driven? Why didn't someone stop me from driving? I was crying now; not for those I had killed, but for myself; for my life that was planned and never to see the light of day. I was crying because of the shame this would cause my father and my mother; my brothers and sister. Would any of them visit me in jail? I would be a criminal; a convict. I could not plan my life anymore as my life was no longer mine to plan. The State of California had control of my life now and all because I was stupid. Did I commit a crime? Yes: I drove whilst intoxicated and in doing so killed 5 people. No, I killed my 5 best friends, not people. My actions snuffed out the lives of beautiful and loving friends with their own plans for the future; their own families to raise: Even now, locked in this room I was already a criminal; a convict.

Nursing staff would enter and check me out regularly; check the diaper I was wearing and change it when it was required. They fed me as I could not use either arm, as one was in plaster at a ridiculous angle and the other handcuffed to the leg of the bed. This would be my life from now on. Chains; hand cuffs and ankle cuffs. Led around, searched and dressed in the finest prison fashions of the day: Incarcerated in a cell with either an iron door or just open prison bars. Why? Because I didn't think: Because I was stupid. It was my act of stupidity that has put me in prison.

Chapter 2

I felt it was late when a young guy, about mid 20's to late 20's entered. He was dressed in a suit and tie and had a brief case with him. He walked over and placed his hand in mine; the one handcuffed to the bed.

"Dieter Faber: I have been appointed as your lawyer by your father. I have the brief here and the police reports. You certainly have got yourself into an awful mess Malcombe. Looking at the charges, you won't ever get out of prison alive. What we have to do is find a way to save some of your life but this might not be palatable for you. I phoned the Prosecutor before I came here and he is willing to negotiate a possible manslaughter charge on 5 counts which might get your sentence down to around 25 years before considering you for parole. Involuntary Manslaughter has a sentence of 9 to 15 years, and if we can get the lighter sentence, it will mean 45 years with a non parole period of 20 years. If you keep your nose clean, you could be out of prison at age 38 or there about: Still time for you to have a life."

"It doesn't sound like much of a deal."

"Would you prefer 100 years and non parole period of 60 years? Not much of a life at 78 years old either." He could see the tears in my eyes. "This was the result of your actions Malcombe and we all have to pay for our mistakes."

"Why me? What did I do to cause this?"

"Youthful stupidity? At your age you think you are invincible and your thoughts don't look at the consequences of your actions. This is reality Malcombe; the reality of your actions."

"Is there any way you can get me off these charges?"

"Not a hope in Hades. Your blood alcohol test came back as 0.207 ppm. That is over 4 times the legal limit. If we went to court today the judge would throw the book at you and the key to your cell into the Pacific Ocean. I will request an adjournment at your arraignment tomorrow as I need more time to study the case and negotiate with the State Prosecutor. You; in the meantime; will be taken to the closest prison with proper medical facilities and remain there until your trial. That might take up to two years. You won't be required to attend the arraignment tomorrow due to your injuries. From this moment, consider yourself a prisoner of the State of California and get used to your lack of freedom. You're going to be locked up for a long time regardless of how good a deal I can do for you."

"Have you talked to my father?"

"Yes, only to arrange for me to represent you. He has told me he wants nothing more to do with you. He will pay your legal fees, but does not want you to contact any of the family in any way."

"I understand." I felt sad knowing that my family would not or could not support me in my time of desperate need of support and love. I was aware too that my father would make sure none of the family would ever know what I had done and where I was. To him I was killed in that crash and that's what he would tell my family; He would even go as far as a mock funeral to ensure no further questions. To the family I was dead and buried, to the State of California I was locked up and forgotten. I'm not sure if death would have been a better outcome for me. I certainly didn't relish prison for 45 years or even 20 years for that matter.

How did I get myself into this mess? I was a good student, clean cut, well presented and no different to any of my peers. Now I was a convict, a common criminal. This would be my life from now on. Even when I eventually managed to get released on parole, I would still be the lowest of the low; a released criminal; to be watched and harassed by the police and feared by those living around me because they only know me as a criminal and not as the youth I was.

I found it hard to sleep as nurses constantly came in and out of the room to check on me. Then the visit was different and my items from my pockets and what little belongings I had, were put in a paper bag and left on the foot of my bed. A short time later two men in prison guard uniforms entered and wheeled me out and down the corridor to a waiting van. I was placed inside and the doors closed. The van was dark and windows showed little as the van started its journey. The journey did not feel long although I did sleep a little as I had been given a sedative before I was taken. I woke as the van came to a halt and I heard the wrought iron gates open and the van move through, then the van entered another area but this time the sound of the gates were more ominous and led into some form of compound. The van came to a halt then reversed to a loading bay. The doors swung open and ahead I could just see a sign: San Quentin Prison. The van had travelled from Los Angeles to San Francisco and I had slept the whole time. There was a clock in the medical section I was taken to and I saw it was about 5.30 and I assumed it was PM not AM.

I was placed into a row of about 12 other beds and saw there was only one other guy right at the other end of the room. A medical staff member came over. He started to check my files, took the paper bag off my bed and took it away. Through my swollen eyes I saw his top had a number on it. Although in white, I assumed he was as much of a prisoner as I was. I never talked to him that first night and saw nobody else until the next day when the supposed prison doctor called into the ward. At least the hand cuff had been unlocked from the bed. I could move my arm and take things in my hand. The wards man still checked me every few hours and my diaper and changed me when needed. The doctor never told me his name and a new wards man had taken over for the day shift.

"The warden will visit you later 264715 and give you a run down on what he expects of you whilst a prisoner here. You will be in this prison ward for about 6 weeks before joining the general prison system. You were arraigned this morning and remanded for 6 months without bail. Your lawyer has called and told us he will visit you tomorrow. Rest while you can 264715 for once you move into the general prison population your days will be filled with work. From what I have seen from your paperwork, you'll be with us for some time." As he turned to go, an alarm went off and he rushed away with the wards man. It was about an hour later when a man was wheeled into the ward, blood covering him everywhere I could see.

Both the doctor and the wards man worked feverishly to stop the flow of blood and finally stemmed the flow and stitched the cuts. They had to cut the prison uniform off him to get to the stab wounds. He was in great pain and you could hear him moaning and screaming out names combined with profanities. The guy at the other end of the ward had not spoken at all since I had arrived. When the panic was over and the wards man was once again free and checking on his charges, I asked about both men.

"You're better asking no questions kid. Answers can upset."

"Why?" I asked.

"Because you don't know prison kid, but you soon will and what happened with that guy there (pointing to the guy brought in covered in blood) will possibly happen to you in the future. So don't ask questions."

"What about the guy at the other end of the ward?"

"He's in a coma after he was attacked and had his head bashed in. He made a pass at one of the guy's boyfriend. He paid for his stupidity and might never be normal again."

"Boyfriend?"

"You are either a boyfriend or 'Bitch' or the Dom or dominant in a relationship."

"Why did you say relationship?"

"When men are locked up for even a few months, they have to get their rocks off kid. It's your ass or theirs and for new kids it's usually their ass that's fucked. You're the new prison cunt; new prison bitch." It sent a chill down my spine as he said that. You always hear of this happening in prisons but as a law abiding person it happens to the socially unaccepted not to you. Now I am the socially unaccepted person and open to sexual abuse. "Just watch your ass and stay out of fights and maybe you might just survive in here. But don't be a hero and if you are put on by a guy, if you don't think you can beat him in a fight, then succumb to his advances. It doesn't mean your queer, just trying to survive."

I received a visit from the police again but I refused to talk unless my lawyer was present and they left. However, when my lawyer did arrive the next day, they were with him and I was questioned again.

"Malcombe Everett; You have been charged with 5 counts of Culpable Homicide. It is my duty to investigate the accident and make a report to the Coroner. To complete my report, I must ask you some questions relating to your activities prior to the accident. Are you willing to answer my questions?"

"My client will only answer questions that will not further prejudice his case." My lawyer stated.

"Malcombe Everett, you recorded a blood alcohol content of 0.207 ppm showing a total disregard for the law and for your passengers. What did you drink, where and in what quantities?"

"Don't answer that Malcombe. Let them do some leg work and find witnesses if they can."

"Ok, then the car. It has been reported that the car was stolen prior to the accident: Where did you steal the car and at what time?"

"You are fully aware that the car was owned by my client."

"On the contrary Mr. Faber: The car was owned by a Mr. Ronald Everett not Malcombe Everett. Mr. Ronald Everett stated in his statement he did not give permission to this person to use the car, therefore the car is classed as stolen and he will be charged later with Grand Theft Auto."

"Did Mr. Everett report the car stolen?"

"Yes this morning. He said he was advised to report the theft. When I asked if Mr. Malcombe Everett was his son, he said he didn't have a son called Malcombe."

"A convenient report? Mr. Everett can now claim the insurance on the car as stolen and wrecked instead of being held responsible for the cost of law suits for the 5 deaths. Those costs will now fall on Malcombe Everett who will be unable to pay and therefore time in prison will be added to cover those costs. May I remind you Detective Sergeant that collusion with Mr. Everett in insurance fraud will not be worth your pension?"

"I don't like your insinuations Mr. Faber."

"I don't like your insinuations concerning my client Detective. The car was owned wholly and solely by my client and although originally bought by my clients father, it was given to my client for his 18th birthday. If Mr. Everett failed to change the ownership papers and insurance details, then that is a separate matter and Mr. Everett should be charged with those offences separately. If that paperwork was altered after knowledge of the accident, then you will have a case of fraud to add to your investigations."

"As the charge has been laid, I must formally charge your client with Grand Theft Auto."

"I suggest you consider that carefully Detective and investigate this closely before charging my client as this could be just the loop hole I'm looking for to remove my client from custody." The head detective huffed and turned and left the room followed by his partner.

"I'm sorry Malcombe, I tried for bail but I knew it would be refused. The serious multiplicity of the charges could not allow you freedom. Your case has been listed for mention in 6 months but the trial will be at least 2 years away yet. In the meantime, you will remain in this hospital section for 6 weeks then moved to the remand section where prisoners are held pending court appearances. I will try and have your case moved up but I don't hold much hope. Now, I need you to tell me everything you remember from the time you left home; and I mean everything. Remember, what you tell me is in the strictest confidence."

"What do you want to know?" I asked.

"What time did you leave home?"

"Roughly about 6.30pm. Dad had just arrived home and asked if I wanted a lift into town. I said no and that I would take the Buick. He agreed and told me not to drink to excess and I assured him I wouldn't."

"So he knew you were taking the Buick?"

"Yes."

"Did you own the Buick?"

"Yes. When dad gave me the car, I signed the registration papers and the insurance papers."

"So why did he report the car stolen by you?"

"You told me yesterday. I'm persona-non-gratis by him and my family. I'm dead so if I'm dead then the car had to have been stolen. A dead person can't drive. If I'm not his son then I must have stolen the car and my name is just a coincidence."

"That's a dangerous game he's playing. To report a car as stolen when it was not is an offence. I have to convince a jury he is your father and knew you had the car that night. You have to decide whether you want to go to a jury trial or plead guilty to a lesser charge and accept the sentence handed down."

"I don't know. What do you suggest?"

"I've looked at what evidence the police have and personally I believe a deal with the Chief Prosecutor is our best bet. If I can get the charges down to manslaughter, then we have the chance to receive a lower sentence. The prosecutor will recommend a sentence and the judge usually will go along with the prosecutor."

"What sentence would you expect me to get?"

"Unless I can get the prosecutor to reduce the charges, then you will have a life sentence with no chance of parole. If I can get the charges lowered to Manslaughter, then 5 charges would be a minimum of 45 years with a non-parole period of 20 years. The time you have already served on remand will count towards your release so you could be out in 18 years. At 36 or 37 years old, you have the chance to start a new life whatever it is. You can never have a brilliant job when you leave here, but any job where you are free is better than the situation you are in now."

"I can't believe I am in prison."

"Kid you're in the shit and nobody to help you except me. I urge you to go for a plea bargain and get the best deal you can get."

"What do you think you can get for me?"

"At best? 45 years with a non parole period of 20 years and that's the best deal I think you will get; but for that you have to plead guilty."

"And if I plead not guilty?"

"5 life sentences: That means you will die in prison."

"I don't really have a choice do I."

"How much did you really drink Malcombe?"

"I had 4 Bourbons at the bar then 6 or 7 Bourbons at the night club."

"Did you eat at all?"

"Not a meal as such, just nuts and bar food."

"That was your first mistake. If you had eaten anything more than nuts, you might have reduced your alcohol content and survived this."

"Please try and get the best deal for me Mr. Faber."

"I will but you better get used to prison lad. This will be your life for many years to come." I shook his hand and he left me to my misery.

Chapter 3

"Word has it you murdered 5 people." the wards man stated.

"I killed 5 people in a car accident, not murdered them."

"Just words kid; you killed them just as much as if you stabbed them to death. You will be haunted by their faces for the rest of your life. Every guy in this prison will know what you did before you ever leave this ward. You will be known as a multiple murderer for your entire life at this prison. People will test you by trying to fight you and they will fight to the death; like this guy next to you. He had over 20 stab wounds from a group who decided he should have been given a death sentence not a prison term. Watch your back kid; you killed 5."

"I didn't do it deliberately. It was a car accident."

"You killed 5 people kid. Now you have to pay for it. Don't look for sympathy either. Every guy in here has his own problems; some worse than others. Some are psychotic so stay away from them. Stay away from the groups and gangs too."

"I'm not into gangs."

"It don't matter kid. The gangs will find you and demand you join them. A guy will like your looks and decide he wants you to share his bed at night, so the gang leader will have their corrupt guard organise your removal to the new cell. You won't have any say in the matter and you will be a bitch boy for a gang member. If they get into a fight in the recreation room or in the exercise area then you will be expected to fight with them and this is when the other gangs can target you."

"Do you have a boyfriend in here?"

"We all have kid, only mine is the bitch."

"How did you get to be the wards man?"

"I was a doctor before I was sentenced to life for the murder of a patient."

"Why did you kill a patient?"

"He had cancer and was in dreadful pain. He had only weeks to live so to help him with his pain, I put him gently to sleep. They charged me with murder. I have no regrets and would do it again if I had to."

"Why haven't you done it to the guy at the end of the ward?"

"He has a chance to live, even if not as well as before. That is definitely murder not Euthanasia. I am all for Euthanasia but not murder."

"What do you expect the guy in a coma to be like when he is conscious?"

"Most likely he will be more child like; little if no memory of his past and might have to be taught to walk, eat, toilet train and generally taught to live again."

"That's awful."

"Not really. When he wakes up he will most likely accept prison more readily as it will be all he will know."

"What's he in for?"

"Murder: He killed his girlfriend and the guy he found her with. He has 20 years to go before he comes up for parole. I doubt he will get it though. He has always been violent since he arrived here."

"Not now he isn't."

The guy who was stabbed remained in an induced coma for 3 days when he finally opened his eyes. He started thrashing around against his restraints.

"Get these fucking straps off me fuckhead." He screamed when the wards man came over to see what was happening.

"Ok Stanley, slow down and take it easy. The straps are there to stop you splitting the stitched areas. You got 20 stab wounds there so calm down."

"When you going to let me sit up."

"Couple of days before the stab wounds will heal enough for you to sit up. In the mean time you will have to put up with me wiping your shitty ass."

"You stay away from my ass you queer fuck."

"Careful Olga: who's calling who a queer? You carry on and I'll fuck you up the ass and laugh doing it while you remain strapped to that bed. Now, let me look at those wounds." He checked out Stanley or should I call him Olga, then covered him up again. "Looking good Olga you'll be up and about tomorrow but in the meantime, you will be strapped to the bed, ok?"

"Yeah I suppose so Doc. Always wanted you to fuck my ass anyway."

"You're just a slut Olga. Here meet my new charge Malcombe."

"He's cute Doc, does he fuck?"

"Careful Olga, he is a murderer of 5 people and more than a match for your ass."

"He looks so gentle too: Mind you I like a man with spirit. 5 you say?"

"5 and he's not so gentle. Vicious mind too." Doc said with a wink towards me. I didn't know if I liked being called a vicious murderer; stupid yes but vicious? I looked over at my new ward mate Olga.

"Why do they call you Olga?" Olga was an African American, big brute of a man; around 6'6" tall, huge arms and legs like tree trunks, a massive chest and a slim waist.

"I was a drag queen before I stabbed my boyfriend. I caught him with another drag queen. He was so beautiful but had a wandering eye. Knowing is one thing but to catch him at it in my bed was the living end."

"Did you kill him?" I asked fascinated

"No but I wish I had. I would still have got 20 years for murder instead of 20 years for Grievous Bodily Assault. Oh

I miss him; he fucked so well. No guy in here can come close to him. They are either too quick or too rough or can't get it up hard enough to get entry to my ass."

"Why do you like male sex so much?"

"Spoken like a true unbeliever. Until you have tried it you will never understand. Don't worry kid, with looks like that you won't have to wait long to find out. Once you are in the general population you will get fucked many times a day and enjoy the taste and feeling of sucking off many men." I cringed at the thought of sucking of a man's cock; a cock down my throat and in my mouth. I couldn't think of anything more disgusting and sickening. My sexual life had been short with my girlfriend Rebecca but my cock was always sated by my right hand at least once a day. Now I couldn't get a fat even if I wanted too; I hurt too much.

It was a week and a half before the guy at the end of the ward came out of his coma. Doc was right and he had no memory of where he was and what had happened. Doc kept the diaper on him for at least another week before deciding to try the toilet for him. He was unsteady on his feet at first, but within 2 days needed no assistance to walk himself. Doc started to question him as to where he thought he was and realised he had no idea he was in prison. Doc told him this was his home and he would be moved into a new room soon so he had friends. His name was Reggie Albright and was in prison for murdering 2 people, and sentenced to life in jail but a further assault in his first year in prison had added a further 15 years to his sentence. Although badly injured in this attack he would not receive an early parole hearing and would still serve at least 20 years; coming up for parole about the same time as I would. It was about 2 weeks after my arrival at the prison when Reggie came up to my bed and spoke to me.

"Why don't you come down and talk to me?" Reggie asked

"Sorry Reggie, I have a broken leg and collar bone and it is hard to walk."

"You're nice and talk to me."

"You're nice too Reggie. You've been asleep for a while."

"Have I? I don't know much."

Why don't you sit and talk to me Reggie and keep me company."

"Yeah I'd like that. Where are we?"

"In prison mate: We did things wrong and they sent us away to prison."

"I heard of those places. They aren't nice places. Will you look after me?"

"Sure Reggie, I'll talk to Doc and see what he can do."

"Can I lay with you?"

"Why?"

"I want to hold you and make you well." I was astounded at what he said but how could I say no. As he laid his head on my pillow, Doc came back into the room and smiled.

"Get to know him Malcombe, he will protect you from the gangs." and walked back into his office. When he came back later, Reggie was sound asleep on my bed with his head on my left shoulder. "Time for you to move Reggie, I have to check him and change his diaper."

"No I will look after him, you go." Doc was surprised at first but then relented. Reggie was not gentle and in fact he hurt me often but he insisted and from that day, Reggie became my constant companion and took the weight off Doc. Reggie just wanted to do things, and be friends. Olga didn't like him and said so. If Reggie went too close to Olga, Olga would lash out with his hand or foot. Reggie even washed me several times a day and massaged my body to avoid bed sores. Doc taught him and by the end of 2 weeks, Reggie was almost as good as Doc.

"Hey Doc?" I called out when Reggie was away in the toilet. "When are they putting Reggie back in the general population?" Doc came over and whispered in my ear.

"Supposed to be next week, why?"

"Any way of organising he stay a while and goes into general when I do?"

"You found a boy friend eh?"

"It's not like that. He is a kid and there are many out there who will take advantage of him. Better he is released with someone he understands and accepts."

"And that person would be you? You fallen for this idiot?"

"Fallen, what in love? No it's not like that but I do feel protective of him."

"You still have two weeks left in here. I'm not sure I can convince the doctor to hold him here."

"You could if he had a relapse, like another coma?"

"What you asking me to do or should I not ask?"

"When he comes out of the toilet, call him over and let's talk to him and ask him."

"He wouldn't understand."

"He would if I talked to him in the way he would understand."

"Ok but nothing elaborate; I've got to convince the Doctor remember." Doc called Reggie over when he reappeared.

"Reggie we are sending you back to the general population on Monday."

"Why, I like it here. Malcombe is here."

"What would you think if you stayed here longer but was asleep again for a week or more?" I asked him.

"Can I sleep with you?"

"Of course you can Reggie." I winked at Doc. "Then when I go back into the general population you can come with me."

"I can? You will look after me?"

"Yes Reggie I will look after you. When the plaster comes off Doc will wake you up and you can help me learn to walk again."

"Ok Doc, then I can stay with Malcombe."

That night, Doc told Reggie that he was going to put him to sleep again. Reggie laid down with his head on my shoulder and Doc injected him with a sedative. Then with great strength, shifted Reggie onto a bed and wheeled him back to his end of the ward. In the documents, Doc said he had collapsed and was put to bed. Each evening when Doc took over the ward, Reggie was injected again. The prison doctor accepted Doc's explanation and left Reggie alone. It was 5 weeks after I had entered Prison when the casts were removed from the collar bone and the right leg. I had not seen my lawyer since he had arrived with the detectives. He chose this day to arrive once again. He smiled when he saw me without the plaster.

"I hope to be walking within the week." I said with a big grin.

24

"Well I have some good news and some bad. The prosecutor has agreed to the lesser charge of Manslaughter but the charge of Grand Theft Auto will stay until they investigate it further. They have also added illegal use of a motor vehicle and dangerous use of a motor vehicle causing death. That will add another 30 years to your 45 years. The non parole period will extend to 30 years and not 20 years but still better than what we started with." I immediately became depressed and I know my eyes watered over.

"Can't you just make this thing go away?"

"Sorry Malcombe; some things just can't be wiped away. You have to wear this and accept your fate."

"But why have they added extra charges?"

"Your father requested you be charged with stealing the car. The prosecutor understands this might fail so has added the other charges to make sure he gets a conviction. If the investigation proves to be a false report and your father is charged, the prosecutor will remove the extra charges. It is the best I could do Malcombe. The detectives are outside now and want to charge you with the extra charges."

"Call them in and get it over with." I said almost in tears. I couldn't understand why my father would do this to me. He and I had always been so close but now it's as if I had never been born. My lawyer got up and called the police in. The usual warning of 'anything you say etc' and I was formally charged with the three new charges. Questions were refused by my lawyer and the detectives left once again empty handed.

"We have to make them find evidence to make the charges stick Malcombe. By answering questions we allow them to gauge your answers with what little they have and in some cases by the way you answer or hold your hands. Investigations are as much observation as receiving verbal answers."

"Have you seen the evidence on these new charges?"

"No, not yet but I assure you we will fight them. However, if we plead guilty to the manslaughter charges we might be able to have the extra charges dropped. But I want them to investigate and find the fraud carried out by your father and others."

"That will hurt my father and family."

"Your father has legally declared you dead Malcombe. You don't have a father. Therefore what we have to do is make sure we find the evidence to prove you are his son. I have already moved on that and got to your birth certificate before it was wiped from the county records. I wasn't quick enough with your school records but not all is lost as I have a friend who can hack into the school computer and retrieve deleted material. I will make you live again and then make sure your father is charged with fraud and tampering with official records. I will also have all those who assisted him charged with him."

"Have you found out when my trial will be?"

"No, it has not been listed yet. Your case comes up for mention on the 8th May."

"It was a lonely Christmas without my family Mr. Faber but I had Reggie here and Olga; but Olga has gone back to general population now. I start physio on Monday."

"Don't give up hope Malcombe; it's surprising what can come out of the blue. I am in constant contact with the prosecutor. He's an uncle of mine so always willing to talk to me.

"Why was I moved to San Francisco and not to a prison in LA?"

"Your father requested it from his friend who is high up in the State Correctional Department. Word is he wanted you far away so your family would never know you were still alive." Now I understood.

Chapter 4

I was anxious to walk again and start to use my right arm, but both were painful and my joints stiff. Reggie massaged my leg and arm trying desperately to get my limbs working. It was 3 days before my leg started to feel better and less painful. My shoulder and arm took longer, more like 5 days but I had run out of time. I had two days before I was to be moved into the general population. Doc told Reggie to get me walking and he started to support me when I tried to walk. My head was spinning after so long on my back and I spewed several times but I did start to walk. I was not too steady and had a pronounced limp but I walked and finally used the toilet for the first time in 6 weeks but my time in the hospital wing was at an end. I was given the prison uniform to put on, the sheets for my bed and two blankets, a small toiletries kit, a towel and finally taken in chains to my new home. Reggie came with me and Doc said he had talked to his friendly guard and tried to get us in the same cell. We were but not as I thought of a cell. The prison was holding about 1/3rd more inmates than it was designed for; 3800 inmates in a prison designed for only 3000. Extra beds were placed into a large hall which had been a gymnasium originally and there were around 300 men cramped into the area in double bunks. We were shown to a double bunk and told to make up our beds.

"Can I sleep with you tonight?" Reggie asked me as we tried to make our beds.

"Let's see Reggie. It depends on what happens and if anyone here objects."

"I can't sleep when you're not next to me."

"You might have to learn Reggie." We helped each other make the beds and then explored our giant cell. There were bench seats around severable small tables at one end and a small TV set. There were toilets and an open shower in one corner. Other prisoners were either lying on their beds or sat at the tables watching TV or playing cards. Malcombe didn't want any trouble so did not talk to anyone. One prisoner made a lured remark as they passed and another asked if Malcombe wanted to suck him off. Malcombe avoided any eye contact knowing he was being watched and eyed off as a possible sex object. It made his skin crawl as he walked around and back to their bunks. Reggie was not overly tall, but still stood at around 6' and had a powerful looking body. Reggie would be a good bodyguard for him. Malcombe wanted to have a shower so asked Reggie to go with him and make sure he was not set on by the other inmates.

Malcombe stripped down and dressed only in his boxer shorts, grabbed his towel and soap and headed towards the shower. As he passed a bunk close to his own, a guy grabbed his shorts and pulled them down. His ass butt naked, several men suddenly appeared as if from nowhere and grabbed him; throwing him onto one of the vacant beds and slamming his head into the metal support for the top bunk. Reggie didn't know what was happening and just stood there and watched as I was brutally raped by 6 inmates. Others stood and watched while others pulled themselves off watching. Now I felt the ferocity of men when their juices were flowing uncontrollably. The pain was

28

high and even the now healed leg and shoulder hurt like mad. My ass felt like it was on fire and I felt cum flowing into me. Then one inmate stuck his cock in my mouth and demanded I suck it but I shook my head no, so he grabbed my head and face fucked me. I thought I would suffocate as I had little or no breathing through my broken nose. What Olga had said didn't feel like that right now and I never wanted to be raped again. When they had finished their fun, they left me lying on the bed and walked away. Just then another inmate approached the bed swearing at me for messing his bed and to get the fuck off. I stood slowly and headed once more to the shower. I had to wash the filth I felt on me and inside me down the drain.

"Why didn't you stop them Reggie? Why didn't you fight them off?"

"You didn't tell me to fight them; you said for me to make sure you were not sat on when you were having a shower." I started to laugh loudly. I needed to really spell out what I wanted Reggie to do for me. My shower finished, I sat and talked to him and then dressed again only in my shorts, then lay on the bed. Reggie lay down next to me and within minutes he was asleep.

"Rico, we got a pair of love birds here." I looked up and saw a small chunky guy looking down on me. He looked like a Puerto Rican with thick black hair and a sallow skin. Another Rican came and stood next to him.

"That's Reggie the fuck that tried to put on with my cock boy. He's fucked now and if the new guy wants him he is welcome to him. Doc says Reggie is a vegetable with a 5 year old brain. Looks like I did him a favour; that's more brain than he had before hahaha." His laugh was like a hyena, high and spine chilling. So this was the guy who kicked Reggie's head in.

"The new guy looks good Rico: Would look good in your bed."

"Nah, Reggie would want to join us; don't have room for 4 of us."

"Mack is leaving on parole next week and you need a new fuckhead Rico."

"Not him, too sweet looking. Let the Aryans have him." Rico then turned and walked away and his buddy joined him. I breathed a sigh of relief. But it was not for long. Within minutes, I was called out again only this time I was taken to the far side of the area near the entry door. The guy who escorted me was covered in tattoos dominated by a large swastika on his forehead; He didn't ask me to follow him, he just grabbed me bodily and took me objecting and stumbling forwards. We reached the end bed and there was a vicious looking guy lying there.

"You're my new fuckhead boy. You will sleep in my bed tonight. Have to do something about those bare arms though. Can't have a clean skin around me; won't do my image any good. Needles, you got a customer." I shook my head no.

"I don't want tattoos and I sure don't want to be your fuckhead boy. Find someone else." I was doing everything against what Doc had told me to survive in this place but being new, I wanted to make my stand clear. It was then 4 guys grabbed me and held me down on a bed opposite and I was stripped. First I was laid on my back and my head held tight. Needles then went to work on my head, and I knew then what was being tattooed there. A swastika! I had to look like an Aryan from a distance and part of his gang.

The needles hurt like hell especially as the forehead has little flesh to absorb the needles and pressure. Needles was quick as tattoo needles and equipment were banned from prison cells in fact anywhere in the prison. The swastika took about 40 minutes of agony to finish. All prison tattoos are black only, as it is too difficult to import colour into the prison but black can be made from many ingredients. Once completed, I was turned over and a tattoo put on my left elbow. Being held down, I could not see what it was. Then my back and shoulders. My body was in huge pain from the tattoos and from the way I was held down as my injuries still gave me great pain. I was finally released after about 3 hours. The bell for chow had rung and the food for this section was brought into the giant cell. Inmates from the kitchen served the food and you ate what was given to you. Reggie grabbed two plates as I could hardly walk from pain.

"A new fuckboy eh? The Aryans have sure done a job on you kid." One of the kitchen hands said.

"Fuck off cunt or I'll smash your head in." I said in anger. I didn't like being called a fuckboy; but of course I was now and no choice about it. I was now in the Aryan Brotherhood for life; distinguished by the tattoo on my forehead and known as a prison inmate by the other tattoos on my body. 5 tattoos had been put on me that day alone, and the leader had said I was going to get more.

We milled around for a while after the food then a bell rang and everyone headed for their beds. I was grabbed and taken to the leader's bed and made to lie down. This was the moment I was dreading. Having been raped earlier, my ass was still very sore and tender. I even had problems sitting on the hard benches around the tables. Then he was there, standing next to the bed, grinning: His tattooed face looking down at me; his arms solid and covered in tattoos as well as his chest, back and both legs. He was a walking piece of tattoo art. I hoped I never had to become what he was and covered in tattoos; but I don't think I will have much choice. I was now an Aryan Brother; choice didn't come into it.

"Lie on your back brother and let this cock find your ass."

"Fuck off and leave my ass alone." Before I had said it, his large fist hit me in the kidney area and his hands had grabbed me and lifted me off the bed. He punched me several times in the stomach and then kneed me in the groin.

"You don't need your balls anyway. That'll teach you to try and use them fuckhead. Now lie face down and I will teach you how a real man fucks." With that said he threw me down on the bed face down and before I could move, he was on me and his cock now covered in spital was probing my ass. He hurt me as he entered my ass. He was large and thick and he stretched me to breaking point, but once he was inside me, he moved quickly and shot his load inside me. It was just at this point when the lights went out and there was an eerie glow from the security lights around the hall. Having shot his load inside me, he collapsed on top of my back; his sweaty body; His masculine sweaty body on top of me and his heavy breathing on my shoulders. After a few minutes, he turned me over and kissed me full on the lips.

"Your ass is tight fuckhead, but sweet. I hear you are in for 45 years, so we will get to know each other real well. You will sleep with me every night from now on."

"I'm not queer."

"I am so you better get used to it fuckhead."

"My name is Malcombe not fuckhead."

"Your name is fuckhead from now on fuckhead. You will suck my cock and be my pussy boy when I want it. You will do my errands and fight by my side. You got a shiv?"

"What's a shiv?"

"A knife or a razor: You got one?"

"No and I don't want one either."

"If you want to live you had better get one. I'll make sure you get one in the morning from Guns, my Sgt at arms."

"Why do I have to have a shiv? Won't the guards find it when they search me or the bed?"

"We have our ways of keeping them safe and handy. You better learn to fight fuckhead as you will be fighting for the brotherhood and often from now on."

"I don't want to fight; I'm not a fighter."

"But you got balls kid and I saw that when you first got here; Doc says you will be a good fighter when we teach you."

"What about Reggie? He is lost not sleeping with me."

"Don't worry about Reggie, He won't last the night."

"You're going to kill him?" I shouted.

"Keep the noise down in there." A guard shouted from outside the bars.

"I didn't say that, you did. Brains take fuckhead here and do what he has to do." I was grabbed and taken to where Reggie was lying and I could see his cheeks where wet.

"You're going to sleep with me now?" He asked as he saw me. Then Brains put a knife in my hand and before I could object, he forced my arm forward and it entered Reggie's body close to the heart area. Reggie just looked at me; eyes wide in disbelief; then blood spurted from his mouth and his eyes closed. He was dead and I really had become a murderer. I couldn't believe what had happened and I turned towards Brains and just looked at him.

"Sorry fuckhead, it had to be done. Nobody has a pussy of their own when Leather's picks his pussy boy. You're just one in a long line of fuckheads. It's his way to make sure you toe the line. While he is happy with you the guards won't know who killed Reggie, but if he decides you are not what he wants, then they will find out and you'll be charged with murder. It's your choice fuckhead."

"But why did he have to die? He was harmless."

"Leather's wanted you totally free and his. Blood in, blood out; it's an Aryan way. If you work out, he has 60 years to go on his sentence and you will be his constant companion both during the day and at night. Blood in means you have to kill to be a member and blood out is for life and only death lets you out."

"I don't relish that."

"You will; you will be feared in this prison, get the best food, all the smokes you want and any drugs you desire."

"I don't smoke, don't do drugs and I'm sure I don't want his cock up my ass for 45 years." As I said that, Brains hit me with his fist into the left side of my face. It held the knife and cut my left cheek as he did so.

"You will learn to smoke, do drugs with Leather's and that cut will leave a good scar; make you look tougher than you are kid. Don't touch it until morning then wash the blood off your face and let it heal by itself; it will leave a bigger scar. The brothers will call you Scar but Leather's will still call you fuckhead."

"This is happening too fast Brains. My head is spinning. I just killed a guy with my own bare hands and I don't even feel remorse. He was my friend yet I don't feel what I did was wrong."

"That's because you knew you had to do it Scar. He couldn't survive without you and Leather's would never let you go. It was necessary."

Chapter 5

They found Reggie the next morning when doing roll call. An investigation was carried out but as the hall was large and the CCTV cameras were set up for an overall view and not individual areas, they could not see the murder or the act itself. They called Brains and I in for questioning as the camera had spotted us walking towards the area after lights out which was an offence in itself, but we both said we had to go to the toilet, and being close to the Latin section, we felt we should go together and not alone. We were both questioned for about an hour but we both stuck to our story and were released back to the hall.

"No problems Brains?"

"No boss, no problems. Scar here did his bit."

"Good. Where have you hidden the shiv?"

"It's hidden down inside the toilet bowl. I wiped all prints off it first. If it's found they can't prove whose it is." I was happy about that. I really didn't want to face a court for murder before I had faced the court on 5 counts of manslaughter. I would live and die in prison.

"264715 you have a visitor." a guard shouted from the bars. I left Leather's and walked over to the bars. "Turn around and put your hands through that gap in the bars." I did what he said and cuffs were placed on me. "Open the doors." he shouted up to the controller high above in the tower room. The doors slid open and I stepped out and the doors slid closed. "Stand facing the bars and spread your legs apart." I did as requested and was then frisked in all parts. My legs were then cuffed together in a loose chain, a belly chain fitted then the chain from my ankles was attached to the belly chain and my wrists then cuffed to the belly chain and the original cuffs removed. I was then escorted through several solid and bared doors into a room and told to sit. I was wearing the normal prison garb of white T-shirt, denim shirt with my number on it and denim pants with ankle work boots. I felt conspicuous in the prison uniform and out of place. I had been in prison for 7 weeks but only in the prison general population for 2 days and had not gotten used to wearing a prison uniform. I felt ashamed dressed as I was but then realised this would be the clothes I would wear for the next 45 years if I didn't get parole. My visitor took about 15 minutes after my arrival before he entered. It was my lawyer Mr. Faber.

"Good morning Malcombe. How are you faring? I see you have been initiated into the Aryan Brotherhood. That won't go down too well at your trial."

"I didn't have a choice Mr. Faber. I was held down and the tattoos put on me against my will."

"They normally are. I asked for you to be placed into the remand section but they have disregarded my request. I will make a complaint but that will go nowhere. The charge of Grand Theft Auto has been dropped but the dangerous driving and driving in a dangerous manner causing death on 5 counts, plus the charge of drunk driving will still stay. Until you sign the paperwork of pleading Guilty to Manslaughter on 5 counts with a sentencing by the judge, the charges will stay. It's the Prosecutors way of saying that if you plead not guilty and get off, he can still put you away for a very long time."

"I killed a man last night."

"You what?"

"They made me do it. A prisoner took me to a bedside, pulled out a knife and grabbed my hand then plunged it into the heart of the guy lying on the bed."

"Have you reported what happened?"

"No and the investigating guards interviewed me and that guy but let us go. They have no evidence to link us to the murder."

"Why are you telling me this?"

"I had to tell someone. He was my friend Mr. Faber but because he was not Aryan they said he had to die."

"What you have said will stay between you and me Malcombe. I talked to your father. You were right; he has declared you dead and your funeral was held one week after the accident. Police are still investigating him for fraud over the insurance claim and also destruction of all records that pertains to you and his being your father. I now have evidence to link you both and your family. However the family still don't want to know you as you are dead as far as they are concerned and they buried you 6 weeks ago. When you finally leave here Malcombe you will be totally on your own."

"I understand. Have you got a date for the trial yet?"

"Your father has interfered once again and the court has transferred your case to the San Francisco court for mention and a hearing date to be set. If you plead guilty then no witnesses will be called and the judge will set sentence. I believe this to be your best option Malcombe and get it over with. It will let you do your time and get out as soon as you can. I will ask the court in San Francisco to set an early date with the promise of a guilty plea and ask for early sentencing. I will ask the State prosecutor to suggest a sentence of 9 years on each count with a non-parole period of 4 years on each count. That will be a sentence of 20 years total Malcombe and will leave you some life to live as a free man."

"Please do what you can Mr. Faber. I know I did wrong and killed my friends, but I am not a murderer Mr. Faber."

"Yes you are Malcombe. You just confessed to me. Should the authorities find out who killed him, you will be charged with Murder and a possible sentence to Lethal Injection, or at least a sentence to life without parole. Keep what you said to me to yourself and if this is held over you in any way by anyone, then do as they say and don't be heroic. They can turn on you at any time."

Chapter 6

I returned to the hall and was frisked again before the belly chain, ankle cuffs and hand cuffs were removed. The door opened and I was shoved by the guard into the hall with the door closing immediately. Brains reached me first.

"Who was your visitor?"

"My lawyer."

What did he have to say?"

"My case has been moved to San Francisco instead of Los Angeles and my father declared me dead and I was buried 6 weeks ago. No hope of any family ever visiting me."

"Dead you say? That's a bonus Scar. Leather's will like that."

"Why?"

"We can use a dead man in our brotherhood: Like having a ghost amongst us hahaha." I hated his laugh but it was true; I was legally dead. We ambled across to where Leather was sitting on one of the benches. He was just sitting and staring into space.

"We have a dead man in our midst leather's; a living ghost. Can't punch through him though like a real ghost hahaha."

"Fuck off Brains; I got to talk to my boy. All you others fuck off too. What I got to say is for his ears only not yours."

The floor cleared around us and he asked me to sit and offered me a cigarette. I took the cigarette and he lit it for me. After a few splutters and coughs, I got used to it and puffed like he did.

"While you sleep with me there are more of those for you. Cigarettes are money in prison so they can get anything you want. Prison has many guys willing to get you mobile phones, a TV when you get a room to yourself, even buy you a room or a young pussy to fuck. Drugs are available for you anytime with enough smokes, so don't give them out unless you want something in return."

"So what do you want in return?"

"Ah you learn quickly. You got a head on you kid and I aim to use it. Brain's has an education but only until he was 13 years old when he went to Juvie. Me, I never went to school, just learnt to fight that's all. You went further didn't you?"

"Yeah, I finished college. Was going to enter UCLA in the spring but the accident has put that in the too hard basket now."

"Not necessarily; ok maybe not UCLA but I might be able to organise you to do university here in San Francisco. You have to do your first year here in prison but then they let you out to attend classes."

"You want me to run drugs don't you?"

"I said you were smart kid. I have a guard doing it now but he retires in a couple of years so I need to replace him. You are my new drug runner kid."

"So what happens if I get caught?"

"Maybe an extra 20 years on your sentence. Nothing you can't handle."

"How'd you know that? I only been in prison for 7 weeks and 6 of that in the hospital."

"You got anywhere else to go?"

"Suppose not. I don't want to get caught. I want to be out of here on parole in twenty years."

"With those tatts and what we are going to put on you in the future, you won't get a job picking up dog shit in parks kid. Better get used to being an Aryan Brother. Outside these bars we can still give you a life."

"Why the tatts Leather's?"

"They make you look fearsome when faced with a fight, especially the Latino's. They hate our guts. The blacks will kill you as soon as you turn your back on them but they still want to buy your weed or smack. They deal with the devil but want him dead too."

"So I'm to be a devil and a fuckboy. You must really hate me."

"Hate you? You got me all wrong kid. After last night, I love you."

"Love, what like a woman or a friend?"

"Both and I reckon we'll be real good buddies before very long. Now, suck me off fuckhead before I flatten that nose of yours further." I knew there was nothing I could do except suck him off so placed my hand on his denim covered crutch, unzipped the jeans and pulled his cock out from his boxer shorts. He was already expecting my mouth as his cock was rising before I had even laid a lip on the head. I closed my eyes as if what I didn't see would not happen, but as soon as my mouth covered his cock, I could taste and smell his cock and crutch. It tasted salty at first but masculine and as I slid my mouth up and down, the taste disappeared and I noticed that my own cock started to rise. Leather's was not a stayer and spilt his load quickly. I was a stayer and my cock was now hard and wanting to be released. As Leather's was spilling his cum into my mouth, I undid my own zip and released my cock from my boxer shorts and started stroking it. It felt so good to be stroking my cock again and it wasn't long before it was gushing wads of cum into my hand.

"Lick your cum off your hand." I looked up at him and he was smiling. "Do it kid and enjoy your own taste. Cum is not slimy and awful. It is you and what you taste like. Enjoy your taste."

"I don't drink cum." He looked at me.

'What do you think you just did with my cock stupid? Now lick that cum off your hand and let me check you got it all, but don't swallow." I was still confused but did as he said. My cum tasted similar to the taste of his cock, salty but not slimy. I licked the cum from my hand then showed my hand to him. He then licked it again, cleaning off what I had missed, then with my mouth still full with my own cum, he kissed me and pushed his tongue into my mouth, releasing the cum to enter his mouth. The cum and his spital mixed and I tasted him once again and my cock started to rise again.

"I thought you said you weren't gay? You could have fooled me kid. You're as gay as I am; you just don't know it yet. I will have to show you how to get the best out of a man." With that he took me down to his bed and pulled me onto it. There he started to move his hands all over me, undoing my shirt buttons and exposing the T-shirt underneath; lifting the T then moving his tongue and lips over my chest; nibbling at my nipples and my nipples were growing harder and felt painful but invigorated. I felt tingling all over my body. Maybe he was right and I was gay, but men and women do that too and their body reacts the same way so that doesn't mean I am gay, just that I react to good foreplay. His lips then reached my lips and he started to kiss me passionately. My eyes were closed and if I had not known he was a man, I would dream of his being a woman. His kisses were strong but passionate just like Rebecca's but the stubble on his face rubbed me and my face became sore. I didn't want him to stop, stubble or no stubble, he was turning me on and had my body on fire. My own body started to react as I would with a woman and I started to take the lead, but his gentle insistence told me to relax and let it just happen. I saw guys standing around watching but it didn't worry me any longer. I was too engrossed in the sexual act with this man. My shirt and T were now off and my zip undone on my jeans. My jeans were being lowered off my hips and my boxer shorts slid down. Leather's was licking me all over including my ass and ass crack. The tongue in my crack sent shivers through me and I felt his tongue entering my ass, gently and then I felt his spital being rubbed over my ass. He then raised my legs over his shoulders putting my ass into the air slightly and then he started to probe me. This time it didn't hurt as much as the night before as my ass was ready and expectant. It wanted his cock inside me and although there was some pain I just wanted him to enter me. Now I understood what Olga had said. I wanted that cock and that pain. I wanted his cock inside me. I needed his cock inside me. Was I gay, I mean really gay? I didn't care; I had a man who wanted me and wanted to fuck me and love me. It's more than my family could do and I really needed love at that time. If that love came from a man then I wanted that love.

He was much slower this time and I could feel his cock moving inside me; gently caressing my inner body. He held himself for as long as he could and my right hand moved on my own cock in rhythm with his body. He finally came inside me and I again gushed cum unto my chest and belly. Leather's finally pulled out and then I realised the other inmates were spraying me with cum from their own sexual climaxes. I was covered in cum, even on my face. When all had finished, Leather's looked at me and laughed.

"You better go clean up unless you want to smell like a man's cock for the rest of your life."

"Is that so bad in here?" I asked

Chapter 7

I was bored by life in prison. We ate 3 times a day, played cards or watched TV, but we weren't allowed out into the exercise area. When I asked Leather's why, he said there were too many of us to control so the just let us mill around in the hall. I wanted to run; run anywhere, even if it was a small yard. I wanted to exercise my right leg and get it back to some form of fitness. Being couped up in this eclectic mix of social deviants was a sure way to a whole load of trouble and that happened after about 2 weeks in the hall.

The Puerto Ricans started it and sought out one of the Brotherhood. They got him alone near the showers and started into him but Brains had seen what was happening and shouted out to Leather's. The Brotherhood was there in seconds and I saw the knives and shivs' come out; blood pouring all over the floor, then the Afros' entered the fray and it became an all in fight to the death. I reacted as soon as Leather's moved, and he threw me a shiv; the one given to me the day Leather's made real love to me. I had never been in a real fight although I had done some wrestling at college but that didn't give me much experience when it came to these guys as most had been raised on the streets and knew how to stay alive. I felt a knife enter my lower back but the guy who had stabbed me then went down hard and I saw Brains had cut his throat. He lay bleeding on the floor. I started to then fight for my life, knowing that I was being targeted as Leather's bedfellow. To know you are being targeted for death is an eerie feeling and makes you fight even harder. I started using my fists and slashing with the shiv and my actions became frenzied. Then an alarm sounded; wailing sounds like an air raid siren. I could hear voices shouting and the stamping of many booted feet. Brains shouted into my ear to wipe the shiv of prints and throw it far away. I did that then fell to the floor and passed out.

"Got yourself into a spot of bother Fuckhead?" I recognised the voice and knew it was Doc well before I was able to open my eyes.

"How long have I been out?" I asked expecting him to say an hour or so.

"2 days. You lost a lot of blood. You're lucky to be alive as I heard they targeted you. You got 13 stitches in your back so don't do any calisthenics for a few weeks ok?"

"When can I get back to the hall?"

"Maybe tomorrow; depends on the Doctor."

"Any one killed in the fight?"

"Only one and from the grape vine it was the guy who stabbed you."

"I expected as much. I saw what Br...."

"Stop right there. If you know who killed him keep it to yourself. I don't want to know and you should be more careful with your tongue in here."

"Sorry Doc, still on a learning curve."

"Yeah well you better study the hand book real quick or you will not live long, Aryan Brother or not."

"How did you know I was with the Aryans?"

"That large swastika on your forehead might have something to do with it."

"I was forced to join and they held me down while needles did his bit."

45

"Yeah figured as much; Tattoos are for life so is being a Brother. Your life is all set out for you Fuckhead whether you want it or not."

"Not." I didn't want to be an Aryan Brother but my choice didn't count. While I was recovering from the stab wound, the head Warden entered and came to my bedside.

"While you are at my prison 264715 you will follow the rules or suffer the consequences and I assure you they are severe. Any breach will postpone any parole hearing by 2 years minimum. You have to have my recommendation for a parole hearing to be called and this fight has already put that in jeopardy, however although you have been charged, you have not been sentenced and are still classed as in remand. Therefore this incident will not appear in your records. The fact that you have already joined the Aryan Brotherhood does not bid good intentions and I will keep my eye on you. From your records I have seen you will be my guest for quite a long time so do not get on the wrong side of me or you will suffer the consequences. I warn you now, keep your nose clean." With that said he turned and walked out of the hospital wing.

"You've made a strong enemy there Malcombe be careful. I suspect he has friends in high places and he is gunning for you."

"I think my father has something to do with that. He would have me killed if he could."

"Don't you think he has already tried?"

"What the fight?"

"Not hard to organise with enough money."

"Fuck, he wouldn't go that far would he?"

"Why not, he has already buried you once, he can afford to bury you a second time as a pauper convict." He was right.

I was released the next day but had to return each morning after I had showered for the dressing to be reapplied. Doc became a good friend over that time and a confidant; but a confidant of thoughts not deeds. We often discussed my father and his treatment of me; his killing me off and maybe attempts on my life in the prison. I knew why he wanted me dead. He feared I would try and contact the family on my release on parole and even maybe on being found not guilty at my trial. He didn't know about the plea bargaining going on and if he had, would not have worried so much. There would be little I could do when finally released from prison. I would look like a convict and by then act like a convict. I would be a totally different person; hardened to prison life, tattooed to put fear into those that saw me and by then an attitude I would develop over time. You couldn't do 20 years or more in prison and come out the same person. No, my life as Malcombe Everett was dead and the Aryan Malcombe 'Scar' Everett had started its long journey to fruition. Leather's was his usual self but became angry when I suggested my father had organised the fight to have me killed.

"You really have upset him haven't you? I suspect this won't be the last attempt either. We had better keep a close eye on you from now on."

"I don't want that leather; I just want to do my time and get the hell out of here. I didn't want your marks but you forced me to have them so it puts me in your league as a criminal and gang member. The Warden came and saw me yesterday and warned me about being a gang member."

"He don't like the Aryans. I'll deal with him later. I have to make a phone call; be back shortly." He moved away from me and I saw he was near the toilets. When he returned, he had a smile on his face. He said nothing.

I got a call out to visit the Warden's office the next day. He told me that my father had died in a car crash the night before on his way home from work.

"I don't have a father; he disowned me when I had the crash and even buried me the following week. He means nothing to me."

"Well he was to pay for your lawyer I was told but now you have no representation: How you going to handle that?"

"I don't care, just plead guilty and let the judge decide my life." I was taken back fully shackled to the hall; strip searched again then placed back behind the bars.

"What happened?" Leather's asked.

"He told me my father died in a car crash last night and jested at my now lost legal representative."

"So the Warden did have some contact with your father. Your father had his finger in a lot of illegal pies Scar. He wasn't as upstanding as you thought."

"Not now he isn't he's worm food now."

"Any remorse?"

"For what he did to me? Not the smallest amount and thank you leather's."

"Why thank me?"

"I know you organised his death and I thank you from the bottom of my heart."

"You're welcome my little fuckboy, now you can get on with your life without your father one step ahead of you destroying it."

I felt no sadness or remorse at my father's death. He deserved everything Leather's had arranged and from what brains told me later, it was a painful death and not in a car accident either. He died in his car but was heavily tortured before the car was sent over the hill; plunging 60 feet and bursting into flames. Brains said the body was unrecognisable and it was hard to identify him. I even shook Brains hand and thanked him. My lawyer did come to see me again about 4 weeks after my father died. I sat in the waiting room in a much happier state of mind, still chained and shackled like an animal and dressed in my killer clothes of a prisoner.

"Well Malcombe we finally have a date for your trial. It is in two weeks time. If you sign these papers pleading guilty to all 5 charges of Manslaughter, you won't have to attend the court."

"I want to attend court."

"But those tattoos will not look good to the judge Malcombe and he may decide to give you a heavier sentence."

"I don't care anymore Mr. Faber. I am who I am and prison has changed me to a criminal and an Aryan Brother not me. If this is what I have to be to survive then so be it; tattoos and all."

"Ok, then I will have you transferred to the court for the hearing on the morning of the case. I will arrange for some civilian clothes to be given to you."

"No, I will go to court in prison clothes. As I said, I am now what you see. How come you are still representing me with my father now dead?"

"He left a large will Malcombe and a separate will in your name to be read out to you on your release from prison. He did, however put in a clause for your defence expenses to be paid."

"I have a sneaky suspicion about that will Mr. Faber but you will never know about it. Please if you can add a few extra dollars to your bill, can you visit me a few times?"

"I often have to visit San Quentin so will try and arrange to visit you as part of the trip."

"Thank you, I appreciate it."

Chapter 8

Once again I thanked Leather's and told him I knew he had made sure my father had covered me in his will and my legal costs too. He just sat there and smiled. Now I had something to look forward to; the trial. Sounds stupid but yes I did look forward to it. It would determine my future and stop the indecision I currently felt. At least I would know the outcome and my mind could become used to the fact that I was legally sentenced and a criminal. It had taken me nearly 3 months to come to terms with my fate and a lot of that had to do with Leather's. Although Leather's was a sadistic bastard; a known killer and vicious to all that crossed him, he loved me passionately. I had never known a love such as his and even though I still considered myself as a straight man, his love was overwhelming and gave me the love and support that would carry me through my time in prison. The Brotherhood was now my family and like it or not, I had to give them my loyalty.

Two weeks seemed like an eternity as the days went by slowly with little to do couped up in the hall. New prisoners arrived daily and were set upon almost instantaneously. I could hear the screams and the sobbing at night. Most were young guys around my age, caught up in the street crime and drug scene. Most would spend the rest of their lives in prison like me and most would end up as a bitch in some older prisoner's bed. Did we all deserve this life? Unfortunately yes. We had broken society's rules and were paying the price. Was society right to take its revenge? I suppose so, but the rules kept changing as society grew and changed. What was acceptable yesterday was a heinous crime today. But I had killed 5 people and even in much earlier times I would have been hanged or even beheaded, so maybe society had also changed for the better.

The big day finally came, and I was called out early, shackled and frog marched to the waiting prison van along with 4 others. The trip took less than an hour and we arrived at the courthouse. We were each led to a separate cell but the shackles were not removed, well at least not from me. I had elected to wear the prison uniform and so would not be released from the belly chain, hand cuffs and ankle cuffs. I would face the judge as a criminal; a common convict that I already had accepted. I lay on the hard bed and pondered my fate. I accepted that I would get at least 45 years with a non parole period of 20 years. I had signed the paperwork to say I would plead guilty. All that was needed now was for the judge to pronounce sentence then I would be transported back to my home of the last 5 months; back to my new family and Leather's. I was first up as I saw the clock in the hallway leading to the courtroom. It was just before 10 am. I was led to a table where Mr. Faber was sitting.

"Are you sure you want to face the judge in prison uniform. I can arrange for a short adjournment and have civilian clothes brought to you?"

"I said no and I meant it. Prison is my life now so I should be who I am, not try and look different just to please a judge."

"Ok, but only say the word guilty when asked how you plead."

"All rise for the Honourable Justice Morgan. The district court is now in session." The judge entered and sat down. We all sat.

"Case 173849, The State of California against Malcombe Henry Everett. The defendant is charged with 5 counts of manslaughter.'

"How does your client plead Mr. Faber?" Faber signalled me to rise and answer.

"Guilty Sir on all 5 charges." I said in a loud voice.

"Very well: Usually I would take time to consider my sentence but the Chief Prosecutor has made a recommendation that I agree with and so ask you to rise. Malcombe Henry Everett, you will serve a sentence of 9 years for each charge of Manslaughter. You have also been charged with dangerous driving causing death on 5 counts and driving whilst under the influence. Council, will you both approach the bench." Both the prosecutor and Faber approached the bench. The judge talked for several minutes before the council returned to their tables. Faber leaned over.

"The judge is going to ask you if you will plead guilty to the other charges. Agree to plead guilty and for sentencing to be given. Do you understand?"

"Yes but why are these charges being laid now? I thought they would be dropped if I pleaded guilty to the manslaughter charges?"

"Please, just do as I ask. You will not be any worse off I promise you."

"Have you had sufficient time to talk to your client Mr. Faber?" The judge asked.

"Yes your Honour."

"Good. Mr. Everett, please stand." I stood. Do you plead guilty to the 6 outstanding charges?"

"Yes your Honour I plead guilty."

"Remain standing. I sentence you to a further 5 years for each of the 5 charges of dangerous Driving causing death and 5 years for driving under the influence of alcohol to be served concurrently with your sentence for the charges of Manslaughter. I post a non parole period of 20 years for the sentence in total. Should you come before the court before your non parole period finishes, you will serve the complete term of 75 years without parole as sentenced as well as any further term sentenced by that court. This court is adjourned for 30 minutes."

"All rise." The judge left and we sat down again. The prison guards stood behind me waiting to take me down stairs to the cells for transportation back to San Quentin.

"Give me a few minutes with my client gentlemen please." The guards stood back but not too far away.

"What just happened?"

"A last minute deal Malcombe. The charges other than the Manslaughter charges were still on the books. You could have been tried at anytime during your sentence on the

53

other charges and would have had maybe another 30 to 40 years added to your sentence. Last night I managed to get the prosecutor to include the other charges in today's trial and have you sentenced immediately but for the sentence to be served concurrently."

"How do you mean concurrently?"

"It means you will only serve the original sentence and not have the other sentence added on after you have served your original sentence. You will still be able to apply for parole at the end of 20 years, however that 20 years is from the date you were arrested and time already spent in prison will be taken into account, so in 19 years and 8 months you could be a free man again. As from now, you have no further charges to answer for." I thanked him and he shook my hand. "Good luck Malcombe, I think you're going to need it." He stood and left the court. The guards then took me down stairs to the cells.

I felt at ease now it was all over. I now knew my fate and accepted it. Faber had fought well for me. I knew he could not make it all go away, but 45 years or 20 years non-parole was the best he could do and he got that for me through his negotiation skills. There was nothing else they could charge me with and it was now up to me to keep my nose clean and get my parole on time. I was happy as a prisoner could be on the trip back to my home; for now that was what San Quentin prison was for me. It was where I had a bed, a love and plenty of brothers who would support and protect me whilst inside.

I arrived at the prison with the 4 other men and we were now processed as real prisoners. I thought I would be taken back to the hall, but I had to go through the whole process that I had missed when I originally arrived as I was injured and in plaster. We were stripped and made to lean over a bench where they checked our anal passage our mouth, and cocks and balls. We were then hosed down then sent to the dusting room where we were painted with a paste on our heads, around our cock, under our arms and any area where hair was present. It burnt badly but had to be left on for 10 minutes before it was hosed off. We were then issued our prison clothes only this time I was given an orange smock and orange pants, I was allowed to keep my boots, and new boxer shorts added to our pile. Bedding was issued and we were then shown to our cells. It was after lights out by the time we arrived in our cell so I just lay down on my unmade bed. I so wanted to be with leather's.

"Aren't you going to join me up here then?" It was leather's voice.

"Leather's, what you doing up there?"

"Waiting for my fuckhead to finally get here. Our gang was moved after lunch into a renovated wing they just opened. No Spics or Latino's here, just us Aryans at the moment." I immediately crawled up and snuggled into him.

"I got 75 years Leather's but a non-parole period of 20 years. My lawyer did a deal."

"Yeah I know. Nice guy judge Morgan, likes the Aryans too."

"What did you do leather's?"

"Made sure your trial date was on his date for court. He would have seen your swastika and made sure you got the minimum."

"Your tentacles spread far and wide don't they?"

"Don't ask and I won't lie to you."

"4 new young guys were put in cells in this block too. I bet they don't remain virgins for long." I laughed but knew it would be the worst night of their lives.

Chapter 9

I was awake early as the noises emanating from the renovated cell block were different from the old hall or dormitory. Although it was quieter for the most part, any noise reverberated through the cell block like an echo. I could hear small screams or a loud admonishment and guessed it came from the cells of the 4 new inmates as they were taught what their new lives would be from now on. I then realised Leather's was awake too. He seldom slept soundly as his ears and brain were always awake ready to react quickly if attacked but in the new cells we were both protected at night by the double door system that had been installed. A solid steel door slid across the bars and a small peep hole had been installed in the steel door for the guards to use for inspections which were every 15 minutes. I suppose we would both get used to this intrusion and noise in time. Leather's didn't like sex in the early morning but preferred to be sucked off. I still had an aversion to sucking a man's cock but it was quite the norm in my life now so became automatic each morning. It wasn't that hard or offensive now; just knowing I was doing it almost instinctively was what annoyed me. I finished sucking him off, and then lay next to him with questions in my mind.

"Have you been told the new regiment for the new cell block yet?"

"We got a quick rundown when we were moved in, but not the full rules and regs. Bells at 0530, ablutions and make beds, then bells at 0600 stand by beds, bells at 0630 and line up for chow; march to chow hall then bells 0700 for finish food and march to outside recreation area."

"We get to go outside?"

"Yeah finally: Its June so should be nice and warm and sunny. Notice you got shorn."

"Yeah, on induction yesterday; I expected it."

"Now you're a real convict young fuckhead its time to make you a fully fledged Aryan Brother. A decent shave will help."

"I shave every morning." I said indignantly.

"I don't mean that bum fluff on your face, I mean this." He said as he rubbed my head. "I want that head clean of hair and shinning like a new pin from now on. Needles has a lot more work to do on you yet."

"What on my head? I don't want to look like needles and the others with tattoos everywhere including up their ass." He then hit me hard across the face and I was reeling from the severity of his anger.

"You will do as I say and like it. You are mine fuckhead and don't forget it. What I say goes and while you are in this prison you will be an Aryan and like it or suffer the consequences." I was subdued for a while as I thought of what leather's had said, but not for long as the first bell sounded and the lights went on.

The cell had its own steel toilet and hand basin. There was a small shelf above the sink for our toiletries and little else. While leather's used the toilet, I shaved; including my head; and washed my face; then we changed over. Our beds made we relaxed for a few minutes resting up against the wall and waited for the bed inspection. The iron door slid open and I could hear the lock on the barred door click unlocked. It too then disappeared into the wall as two guards entered the cell. We stood at attention.

"Morning Leather's, Fuckhead; hope you slept well in your new home? We went to no expense to make this a comfortable and luxurious home for you both."

"Morning Hairier I suppose you don't want a fuck this morning?"

"By you? No thanks, don't want to catch any diseases I can't cure."

"I can cure that easy with a little bloodletting."

"Ha, I'm sure you could. Cook says there is a package for you. Fuckhead has been detailed as a kitchen hand so he can collect it later."

"Thanks Hairier, I will explain it to him later."

Inspection over, the bell signalled again and we all lined up for head count before heading down to the mess hall. This would be my first time eating in the mess hall. Head count done, we were turned to the right, then 300 set of feet pounded the steel grill floor and steel steps down to the ground floor. We had to march in line and in step, and were padded down before exiting the block and then headed for the mess hall. We all lined up at the servery and food was sloped onto a steel tray with two slices of bread. The food was porridge, slimy looking and as cold as ice. 'It will line the stomach' the server said as he smiled. He was a young guy about my age but Afro. As me moved to grab the bread and a mug of tea, the head cook came over to talk to Leather's.

"Harrier tell you there's a package for you?"

"Yeah and young Fuckhead here will get it later when he is sent down to you for work as your new dishwasher."

"He know what he has to do?"

"Not yet but he will by the time he gets here." We then moved over to a table as directed by one of the guards.

"What does he mean know what to do?"

"We got an hour's rec time after this so tell you then." Leather's said no more. We ate quickly as another block was due to move into the mess hall 15 minutes after us. I barely had time to drink down the tea before the bell sounded again. I quickly gulped down my remaining tea whilst standing and nearly choked.

"Got to learn to eat and drink quicker lad." Leather's said while laughing. I tried to respond but all I did was splutter. After we joined a line up heading towards the door, there was another young guy at the door standing next to a large tub of soapy water and as each prisoner moved past him, they rinsed their tray and mug and put them wet on the pile at the door. I did the same, and then we were directed towards another door, patted down again and moved out to the outside recreation area: Warmth, sunlight, the sound of birds and smell of new cut grass. It was heaven after spending the last 6 months couped up inside those walls. Leather's and I moved over to the left side of the rec area away from the small weight training cage. The body beautiful headed for the weights and to show off their muscles and how many weights they could lift. These were the real queers of the prison system. Then I saw those who were the fags of our block; the guys who dressed to show off their bodies with tight denim to show off their ass and cock bulge, or those who had managed to get a woman's blouse smuggled in: The 'queens' of the prison system. They paraded themselves around the area away from the Latino's and Afro's into a corner of their own. They stayed with the sexual offenders, the peddo's and the geeks. Leather's explained the groupings to me.

"After lunch, you will be taken down to the kitchens and start work as a dish washer. Cookie has a couple of packages for you. One you have to swallow and the other push up your ass. Each has a string attached so make sure you swallow the string and all. You will make yourself vomit when you get back to the cell so the string can be pulled and the package recovered. It will be easy to swallow as it is a filled condom. The second is a condom too but you must push it all the way in and the string must not be able to be seen. Don't be too rough as if you break the condoms, you will be dead before we can help you."

"What's in the condoms?" I asked stupidly.

"Not a question I would have expected from you fuckhead."

"Oh, ok, I understand."

After lunch of tasteless watery mash potatoes, tasteless peas and gristly meat stew, I was called out and taken to the kitchen. I was put to work washing the pots and pans and huge boiling pots. The water was scalding but no protection was given. The soap used was quite caustic and my hands were raw quickly. I was given a pair of white coveralls; white rubber boots, a white drill cap and a mouth cover to stop sneezing or coughs' entering food or utensils. I was near to completing the huge stack of pots when the cook came over to me.

"Come with me." He said softly almost as if aside. I followed him into the cool room. He went straight to the chicken stack and pulled out a chicken then reached inside it and pulled out 2 condoms. Each had string attached as Leather's had said.

"Swallow this one." I looked at him. "Now, quickly, don't think about it just do it." I took the condom and tried to swallow it but I kept gagging. He then grabbed it from me, then opened my mouth and pushed it down my throat. I thought I would die; but it went down and he then pushed the string into my mouth. "Swallow the string before someone comes in."

"How am I going to get that up my ass?" I asked.

"Remove your coveralls and bend over." He said

"What if someone comes in?"

"It'll look like I am fucking my new dishwasher won't it?" I did as he said, and he grabbed an amount of lard that was in the cool room, smoothed it around my ass crack then pushed the condom inside me. It wasn't as hard or as painful as I thought it might have been. One quick push and it entered easily. He then told me to push the string well up inside myself which I did. I felt the condom would fall out as I straightened and put my coveralls on again. It took a few minutes before I felt comfortable enough to try and walk. I kept clenching my ass to stop it from sliding out with all the grease around my ass crack.

"It feels like it wants to slide out." I said to cookie.

"You'll get used to it. It's almost time for you to return to your cell. We have other prisoners coming in to do the diner shift." Dressed, I moved back out to the dish washing station and finished off the small pile of pots, always clenching my ass cheeks together. The bell rang and I moved into the store room and removed the boots, hat and coveralls and dressed back in the orange smock and pants. I was then called out, shackled and returned to my cell. It was Harrier that escorted me back.

"You stuffed fuckhead?" He asked. At first I didn't understand what he meant then it dawned on me.

"Yes and I am finding it hard to hold it up my ass."

"You'll get used to it a fine fuckhead queer like you." I objected to being called a queer. I wasn't a queer, just Leather's fuck boy that's all.

Leather's was waiting for me when I returned. I could smell the earth on him. He had been detailed to work in the vegetable garden. I liked the smell; it made him smell masculine: Shit I was starting to like the smell of men now. The longer I stayed in prison the more queer I would become even to the point of enjoying being queer. I hoped not but I didn't hold up much hope of ever being straight again.

"You got the gear." He asked as soon as I walked into the cell and my shackles were removed.

"Yeah: For god sake get the gear out of my ass first, I feel it slipping all the time and my ass cheeks are sore from clenching them."

"I'm not putting my hands up your ass kid, that's your job so be quick about it and do it over the toilet in case any shit falls out with it. When it's out, wash it properly." I did as he said and stuck my fingers up my ass and felt around until I felt the string then tried to grab it, but it eluded my first few attempts but I finally got it. I pulled the string out, then pulled hard and the condom finally slipped out, but the pressure of the condom felt like a big fat turd you had been straining on for the best part of an hour, but of course it only took a few minutes. I washed it quickly and gave it to leather's. Then I had to make myself retch. Fingers down my throat, I finally managed to bring up the string again and once more pulled the string and pulled the condom from my stomach. I think the stomach condom was the worst. It made me feel queasy for several minutes. Washed, I gave it to Leather's then lay on the bed to settle myself down.

"Good job Fuckhead. It gets easier the more you do it: Never been caught yet." The next day when we entered the recreation area, Leather's walked into the centre of the square and had me next to him. Then I saw the head of the Latino's and Afro's do the same each with one of their men. They all met in the middle and Leather's told them they could now buy the best 'Crack' 'Heroine' or 'Smack'. Each bought a carton. Leather's slid the drugs over and they parted company quickly before the guards saw the meeting. When we had reached our corner, I asked what he meant by carton.

"Each group has bought a sample of the drugs for a carton of cigarettes. The canteen holds the cigarettes for everyone as well as a few items like T-Shirts, joggers, shorts etc as well as sweets, cookies, tea and coffee. If you got enough money in your account, you can buy anything. You get paid each week into your account for the work you do. Don't expect to get rich. Most work pays maybe $3 to$5 a week, enough for maybe a pack of smokes and a few biscuits. If you have relatives who visit, they can ask for money to be added to your account but only small amounts."

"Would I have much in my account?"

"You've worked 1 day kid, maybe 50 cents. Don't forget kid prisoners are the poorest people in the whole US of A."

Chapter 10

It was about 3 weeks after I had been sentenced when my life came crashing down around me. In the whole time I had been in prison from the first day I awoke after the crash I had no remorse or emotions about my plight. I understood the ramifications of what I had done and accepted what punishment would be handed down. Even when the Judge sentenced me to 75 years in prison, I accepted my fate. But today it all came crashing down. I started crying uncontrollably during the night and even during the day I broke down and just slid to the floor down the closest wall. I just couldn't help it. It was as if my life had become unliveable. Leather's tried to console me but I threw him away from me, then it happened. One of the gang started to jibe me as being a cry baby and I lost it. I sprung across the table where we were sitting and grabbed him by the throat, pushing him to the floor, and then I just started to smash his face in with my fists, throw after throw, and fist after fist. I knew I was hurting him but I just had to hurt him more. It took 3 guys to get him away from me then the guards arrived and took me down to slots. I didn't remain there long: As soon as the door closed behind me, I started to lay into the concrete walls with my head and fists. The doctor was called and I was removed to the psychiatric cells and strapped down. I screamed and shouted and cried; I couldn't stop. The doctor then entered the cell and injected something into me and I was out like a light. When I came too, Doc was standing over me.

"How are you Fuckhead?"

"What happened?"

"You lost it kid. You beat up Gruber and left his face a bloody pulp."

"Why Gruber? I get on well with Gruber?"

"Who knows the workings of the mind kid? Did he say something to you?"

"I really don't remember Doc. What's going to happen now?"

"A psychiatric assessment then based on the results they will decide what's next."

"Am I a nut case?"

"No I don't think so but I think you should join one of our groups and just let it all out kid. You've bottled it up long enough. It has to come out sometime and looks like it now has. I will talk to the Doctor; he will be here in about an hour."

"Are you going to release me from this fucking straight jacket?"

"No, only the doctor can order that. He put you in that and put you out for 2 days."

"Why?"

"So your mind could rest and get over what was causing you to explode."

"Being in here is what made me explode. Man, I was a normal everyday guy then 'Bang' I'm in prison for 75 years. What do you expect my mind to do?"

"Everybody here was a normal guy once then "Bang" ended up here."

"Yeah but most were destined to be here anyway."

"Were they? Who says? You or types like you and your dad? Who's to say that born in a different street or neighbourhood would have seen a different outcome? Did being born into a poor home where the parents were unemployed or the father cleaned streets for a living make his life less of a chance than you in your rich family and rich neighbourhood. Was he born with any less brains? If you had been born in his house instead of your own, did it give you more chance to remain out of prison because you were smarter? No it is where you grow up and the people you have as friends and neighbours; the guys you gang up with so you can live and survive. Don't come the high and mighty with me Fuckhead. I came from the right side of town and became a doctor but I still ended up "Bang" inside this prison because I fucked up."

"You deliberately killed someone."

"No, I got caught fuckhead; I got caught just like you did." As he said that he thumped a needle into my arm and walked away. I started to feel drowsy then must have fallen asleep.

"How has he been Doc?"

"Quiet as a lamb: Had him chatting earlier before I gave him his 6 am jab. He doesn't even remember what happened. I think the stress of what has happened to him just came home to roost. His emotions finally caught up with him."

"Yes, I agree. You can release him from the straight jacket and let him eat normally and we'll hold him for another day and see how he is." With that he was gone, and Doc started to undo the buckles on the straight jacket.

"You hear most of that Fuckhead?"

"Yeah most of it: Good to be getting this fucking contraption off me."

"That contraption saved your life kid. You still have some nasty head wounds and your knuckles might be sore for a week or so."

"Head wounds?"

"You don't remember bashing your head against the concrete walls of the cell?"

"No I don't or hitting anything to cause this." I held up the hand as it was released from the restraint. "I must have been out of my mind to do that."

"You were: You were out of control and berserk. It took 4 guards to subdue you and two more to get this jacket on you. I think you injured a couple of them too."

"Bad?"

"No, just a few bruised shins and egos."

"When can I go back to my cell?"

"Maybe tomorrow but I'm not sure you will be welcome."

"Why because of what I did to Gruber?"

"Yeah: He is still in a real bad way. It was touch and go for a while. The warden will deal with that later. Looks like you will lose some non-parole time too."

"Fuck I just can't stay out of trouble can I?"

"I reckon you were born trouble Fuckhead." I was left in the padded cell for another day then released back to my cell. I had to report to Doc each morning after breakfast, after lunch and after evening meal for medication. They kept me doped up for 3 months until the Doctor was sure I wouldn't commit suicide.

I felt the icy stares as I was escorted back to my cell; my head and hands still bandaged. Leather's was not there as he was still in his work area and I just lay on the bed waiting for him. Several guys passed by and gave me looks that could kill before 3 appeared in the doorway. They just stood there, their menacing looks making me want to run but there was no exit and nowhere to run. It was just as they started to move into the cell that I heard a familiar voice.

"Going to say welcome back boys are you?" It was Leather's from down on the ground floor. They stopped, looked towards the doorway then back at me. Leather's then arrived at the door.

"You're all idiots. That boy has more guts in his little finger than you all have put together. If I was in a fight I'd want that kid by my side. Now fuck off and find something to entertain your feeble minds like find a Latino in the shithouse and kick his brains in. If I see anyone even close to this kid I will knife you myself. Is that clear?" They all murmured then left the cell and Leather's came in. "Heard you tried to escape by using your head. You fucking idiot; you know the Warden hates you and you give him the opportunity to take some non-parole time off you. He's been itching for you to fuck up and now you've played right into his hand. I don't know what it is between you and him but he has your life in his hands bitch and he has more chance to squeeze it now."

"I think my father and he were friends and when I was sent here it was on my father's request through him."

"Thought as much: He's as crooked as a bent stick. Wish I could convert him my way."

"No chance but I would love to know what arrangement he had with my father."

I became quick and quite adept at swallowing the condoms and forcing the other one up my ass. After a few weeks it was quick and natural: The same too with regurgitating and flexing the ass to remove the condoms. My trip to see the Warden was also quick. I doubt I was there for more than 5 minutes; charges read of 'Aggravated Assault' and 5 years added to my sentence and loss of non-parole period of 5 years also. I was never going to get out of prison in my lifetime. Loss of privileges for 6 months didn't matter as

68

Leather's supplied me with all the privileges I needed but I forgot about my application to study at State University of San Francisco for an Open University course to study Law as my major, and social studies as my second. The Warden had to approve all outside studies, even though all first year studies were carried out inside the prison in a special class area.

My request was denied and an official letter from the University also denied my request stating that no record of my college degree could be found. I remembered what Faber, my lawyer had said about my father trying to rid his life of every bit of evidence I ever existed. I had not seen Faber for 2 months. I would ask him to see what he could do next time he visited the prison. In the meantime, I continued with my work in the kitchens, although while my hands were bandaged, they allowed me to wear gloves. My life consisted of eat, work, run drugs, get more tattoos, get fucked and sleep; pretty busy day really.

I had stopped taking the medication now and I was more settled with my prison life. I had stopped dreaming of ever getting out and living some form of life outside. 10 months in prison had changed me; I could see the changes occurring. I was more aggro in my attitude, stood and walked like the Brothers with a swagger and fought like a demon when the fights broke out. In those 10 months, I had also killed 2 people other than Reggie. They were druggies who hadn't paid their bills who Leather's felt were liabilities and snitches. I had no remorse about any of those I killed. They had been safe kills, set up by all three leaders of the prison gangs. It was safer to have all 3 gangs agree than do it alone: No recriminations, no revenge killings. I had become Leather's right hand man and his confidant: His killer.

Tattoos covered most of my arms, legs, back and chest with my neck and the head being worked on. I didn't like the look but had no say in it. Leather's said do it and needles did it. I just sat and absorbed the pain. That's what prison is all about; dog eat dog, pain, suffering, humiliation and not just by other prisoners either. The guards had their own ways of doing just the same. They knew if there was something you desperately wanted and they would either make you sweat for it or deny it totally. It was their way of saying you depended on them for your living breathe.

Leather's and I were lying on our bed together waiting for the morning bell to get up when the whole building began to shake and the shelf holding our toiletries came crashing down. Dust and plaster started to fall and leather's and I shot out of bed and hid under the bottom bunk. The earthquake lasted for several minutes before it died down and finally stopped but small quakes continued for several hours. It was then I realised how utterly we were dependant on the guards for our lives. Should a fire break out or a large earthquake hit, would they let us out of our cells or just let us die? I don't want to find out the answer to that question. Guards started to check on prisoners and eventually the lights came on and a roll call was called and we all lined up outside the cells. Two prisoners had been injured and were taken to the hospital wing. None were from the Aryan Brotherhood.

It was the following day that Faber came on a visit to San Quentin. I was called out and once again, shackled before being escorted to the interview room. I was so glad to see him and said so.

"Mr. Faber, my application for entry to State University was turned down because there was no record of my college degree, in fact no record of me ever existing."

"I said I had some records Malcombe and I think I have what you need. It is too late for this year's intake but I will make sure your application goes through next year. I have had some new evidence come to light but as you pleaded guilty I don't know if a court will look at it." I became angry.

"You told me to plead guilty; you told me."

"Calm down Malcombe; I agree I did, but based on the evidence it was your best bet. The court will not allow an appeal based on new evidence on a trial where the defendant pleaded guilty. However, should that evidence lead to a conviction of another person who was also involved with the investigation of your case, then the court can demand a new investigation and can overturn your conviction."

"Mr. Faber please don't get my hopes up. I am just coming to terms with my lot in life. Please don't make me go crazy now."

"Even if I could make this happen Malcombe, it is highly unlikely anything would happen within the next 5 to 10 years. Our court system is very slow."

"Do you have control of my money?"

"Yes, but legal costs took most of it."

"Can you have $200 put into my prison account please? I want to buy a pair of joggers and a few T-Shirts."

"I am only allowed to put a maximum of $50 at a time, but I will see what I can do."

"The Warden was in cahoots with my father. It was he who demanded I was taken to San Quentin prison and not a prison in LA. I think he is corrupt."

"I know he is Malcombe but it is hard to find any evidence against him as he covers his tracks well." While we were talking a guard came over and talked to Mr. Faber and told him I had another visitor. "I thought you said you had no family or friends who would visit you here?"

"I don't."

"Well there is a young woman waiting to visit you. I will see you on my next visit and try and see what I can do about the money." I shook his hand as best I could do with the shackles on and he left.

Chapter 11

I sat for about 5 maybe 10 minutes chained to the floor of the interview room waiting for this visitor. When being interviewed, they chain you down to the ring set in the floor as some inmates can get violent especially towards police. The table and inmates chair are bolted down also so they cannot be thrown. I wondered how a woman was able to arrange visitation rights without my invitation and request. Faber was on my list of visitors but that's all. The door opened and a shortish blond woman similar in age to me entered and sat opposite to me but firstly she kissed me and gave me a slight hug. She was a bleach blond, about 5'3" or 5' 4" tall and although dressed well did not show too much of her cleavage or body shape.

"Hi Malcombe, I'm Bonny-Sue Reiter. Dad asked me to call and visit you. He arranged this for me. He didn't exaggerate; you are a good looking guy."

"What tattooed all over my body and head? You like this?"

"Yeah I like it."

"Dad? Who is your dad? Don't tell me, Leather's, right?"

"How'd you guess? He has plans for you Malcombe."

"I don't want his plans. I just want to do my time and get out of here."

"Did he force you to get tattooed or did you want them?"

"What do you think?"

'Yeah well he must like you. Did you have blonde hair when you got in here?"

"Yeah the typical Aryan boy; blonde hair and blue eyes: Why do you ask?"

"I am naturally blonde; oh don't worry about the bleached look, I change my hair colour more often than my knickers." She started to laugh and I was enraptured by this young woman and my groin started to react.

"What's Leather's got up his sleeve?"

"He asked me to check you out and see if you were good husband material."

"Yeah and am I?"

"Sure are. My first husband only lasted 3 months, just long enough to put me in the pudding club then shot off. Leather's hunted him down and had him killed. That was 4 years ago and Jazz is now just 4."

"Jazz?"

"Justin my kid. All the guys down the Aryan Brotherhood Chapter call him Jazz."

"You let him associate with the Aryan Brotherhood?"

"Why not his granddad is one and I hope his new dad will be too."

"You believe in White Power and all that shit?"

"No, but dad is the leader of the Aryan's here at San Quentin and Chapter Leader for San Francisco, so as his daughter I have to show some support."

"But your son? Do you want him associated with them and looking like them?"

:He could do worse."

"I doubt it."

"So do you want to get hitched?"

"What? Don't I have any say in this at all?"

"Sure you do, but when it's time for parole, being married goes a long way, and I promise to visit and bring Jazz along too. It will give you something to look forward to while in here."

"I will talk to Leather's and he will let you know I'm sure. I must admit you really turned me on when you kissed me."

"Dad said you were straight. Don't worry; I know you are dad's bum boy. He wouldn't be doing this for you if you weren't."

"You don't care if a man fucks my ass in here?"

"No and neither should you. It's part of what happens in here. It doesn't mean you're queer just a good looking guy."

"Why did your husband leave you?"

"He was always violent towards me. I nearly lost the kid when he found out I was pregnant with Jazz. He punched me in the belly and slapped me around. The head of the

San Francisco Chapter found me and told dad. Dad told him to find and kill him. They found him hanging from a tree and announced it a suicide. Now I am a widow."

"I can't understand why he wants me to marry you?"

"You and I will produce a good Aryan boy to take over the Chapter from him when he dies; blonde haired and blue eyed."

"You're a beautiful woman Bonny-Sue so why marry me? I have no job prospects when I eventually do get out and I am likely to give Jazz nightmares every time he sees me."

"What the tattoos?"

"Yeah."

"He already has more than one on him. Finger's puts them on him each birthday. He loves tattoos and always asks for more but Fingers told him he can only have one each birthday until he is 18 years old. They are small and hidden when he is dressed, but he is a tattoo demon and I reckon he will have more than you by the time he is 20 years old."

"Can I see you again?"

"I'd like that. Dad will sort the paperwork out for you and next time maybe I can bring Jazz with me."

"Does he know his dad?"

"No, I just tell him his dad is in prison. Dad always said he'd find me a good husband."

Chapter 12

I couldn't see myself a married man with kids. I was just a freak now; in prison I didn't really stand out but outside I would be the laughing stock of San Francisco. No employer would hire me and social security would only last so long before we found ourselves sleeping under a bridge somewhere. I talked to Leather's when I eventually got back to the cell after my work duty.

"What you got in mind for me Leather's?"

"I want you to marry my daughter. I know you're straight kid and Bonny-Sue needs a good man to look after her and Jazz. You won't be wanting for a job outside lad as I have contacts and the Aryan Brotherhood does have legitimate businesses you know."

"How can I get married while stuck in here?"

"I have contacts and might even manage to arrange a conjical visit for you on the wedding night."

"What here in the prison? Sleep with her?"

"Well you already sleep with me, so yeah, with her."

"One night of sex isn't going to allow her to fall pregnant and produce you an Aryan heir?"

"Maybe not, but your sperm can. I will get a sample of your sperm sent each week so she can insert it herself. I'll get you a family yet kid. Now fuckhead drop em, I'm going to fuck the ass off you."

True to her word, Bonny visited every Saturday or Sunday. It depended on the prison visiting list as to what day she could be fitted in. Leather's filled in all the paperwork needed to allow Jazz to come with her and just before Christmas, she arrived with Jazz. He was a good looking kid and we met in the usual visitor section. As Bonny entered, she pointed me out to Jazz and he raced over to me and I picked him up and hugged him.

'Dad, dad is it really you?" I looked at Bonny and she nodded.

"Yes Jazz it's really me. Boy you grown big and your mum says you got a tattoo."

"You want to see it?" He asked excitedly.

"Yeah I want to see it." I tried to sound excited like he was and he quickly rolled up his sleeve. There it was; a WP sign with Aryan Brotherhood tattooed round the base of it. It wasn't big but it definitely showed up on his very white skin. "Did it hurt when Finger's tattooed it on you?"

"Yeah, some but I didn't cry dad; honest."

"You're a strong tough kid Jazz and I'm proud of you. How you going at school?"

"I hate school." He said with a pouting expression on his face.

"School is the best thing for a member of the Aryan Brotherhood Jazz. Most of the members of the Brotherhood have got little or no education and they need men like you and your grandfather to lead them and make sure they are treated right. You will be a leader of the Brotherhood one day so you have to be the best at school, the best fighter and the best man in the house to look after your mum."

"Aren't you coming home to look after mum?"

"One day yes, but it might be a while so you better look after her for me or Leather's and I will be after your hide."

"Ok but I still don't like school."

"You don't have to like it Jazz just be good at it, and if I hear you are the school bully then I will tell fingers not to give you any more tattoos."

"You wouldn't do that would you?"

"I killed 5 people, so why wouldn't I do that?"

"Mum said you killed 8. Is she lying?"

"No but 3 were in prison and they don't count. Nobody in prison counts kid."

"Will I go to prison one day too?"

"I hope not kid. It's not a good place for a kid."

"You were a kid when you came here?"

"Yes and look at what it's done to me. No, you must stay out of prison Jazz, now sit there and let your mum and me talk for a while."

"Ok." He sat in the chair opposite me and next to Bonny.

"You told him I'm his dad; why?"

"He has to have a dad Malcombe and dad says you agreed to us getting hitched."

"Yeah he talked me into it. Please don't misunderstand; I am flattered you want to marry me; me looking like a nightmare."

"Stop saying that. I love the way you look and so does your son. He was so excited when I said he could come today and did he shy away from you when I pointed you out? No he didn't. As far as he is concerned you're his dad and a boy always loves his dad. He doesn't care about your tatts; in fact I think he would have been upset if you didn't have them. Every uncle or friend he has in the Brotherhood is as tattooed as heavy or heavier than you are and he has no problems with them, so why with his dad?"

"Ok, ok, I get you. I just ain't comfortable with them yet. If I had decided to have them done myself then that would be different but I didn't. If my life had not been turned upside down, I would never have had a tattoo ever in my whole life?"

"I know but you do have them and I like them. I like them, Jazz likes them and I know the family will like them."

"Family?"

"Yeah my mum; She has more tatts than you do. Leather's always liked tattooed women. Got 3 brothers too and the eldest is coming to see you next week with me. I got the paperwork through yesterday so he can visit. Mum and the other 2 brothers have been put on your list now so they will all come at some time or other. All 3 brothers are in the Brotherhood and they want to meet their new Chapter leader when Leather's dies."

"Dies? He has 40 years left before he can apply for parole."

"He will be dead within 2 years Malcombe. He has cancer and it's inoperable. He won't have Chemo so he has already passed the Chapter over to you. That's why he wants us married and soon. He also wants you to do the studies at University so you can guard the Chapter. You will need all your skills to keep the Chapter going Malcombe and the Brotherhood alive and together."

"Why me Bonny? I'm just a skinny runt who got drunk and caused 5 people to die."

"No Malcombe, you are a man who killed 3 men to make sure the Brotherhood stayed on top in a place where everyone is trying to be on top. You have the balls to make hard decisions Malcombe and that's what's needed as leader of the Chapter. My brothers will make sure Leather's wishes are kept. It makes no difference that you are younger; you are smarter and Leather's thinks you are more ruthless too. You are the smiling assassin Malcombe; a man to be feared."

"Fuck, I'm a scared little runt who does what he's told that's all."

"So you are marrying me because you were told?"

"No, don't be like that. I agreed because I love you. It has been a gradual acceptance of love as I never felt that a woman could ever love me being in here and the way I look."

"You really mean it? You really do love me?"

"Yes I really do love you and you squirt. Come here and give me a big hug." Jazz came around and as I hugged him a guard came over and told me to stop or my visitors would be asked to leave.

"He's my dad and I love him. I haven't hugged him for a long time mister. He's my dad."

"Ok, but only 1 hug and then you can hug him again when you leave; ok?"

"Thanks mister." and he hugged me hard.

"When do you think we should marry Malcombe?"

"New Years Eve is a Saturday. Let's make it December 31st. I want all your family here when we make it official. I'm sure Leather's can make it all happen."

"I'm sure he can. Do you mind if I dress in white?"

"I would expect no less of you. Mind you I might clash dressed in orange." We both laughed. "And you young man will be my best man."

"What's a best man?" He asked

Chapter 13

As expected, Leather's made all the arrangements. The service was to be held in the visitor section after normal visitor hours had ceased. The prison Chaplin was organised to carry out the service and the visitor list was small but intimate. Mr. Faber; Bonny's mum (Leather's wife): His eldest son Brian: His second eldest son Graham and his youngest son Billy and of course Leather's. I met Bonny's mum a week before the wedding on Christmas Eve and true to what Bonny had said, she was definitely the tattooed woman and would not have been out of place in the Circus. But she was a wonderful woman and if my mum could have seen me now, she would shriek with horror and disown me. But you can't disown what is dead. I would have loved to have invited my own family but being dead made that an impossibility.

I was granted permission to wear a suit and tie to the wedding and it was supplied by the prison Chaplin. I was about his size and it was one of his black Chaplin suits. The permission had come too late for me to buy a new suit. The one proviso was that my ankles were to be cuffed but my wrists were allowed to remain cuff free. Mr. Faber bought two wedding rings for me and brought them to the prison on the day of the wedding. Unbeknown to me, Leather's had arranged a special gift for me; a night sleeping with my bride in one of the special minimum security houses on the prison grounds.

Jazz was so excited when he saw me and said he knew what he had to do with the ring. He was 4 years old but a very knowing and active kid. If I had had a kid of my own I would hope he was just like Jazz. The service was not very long as the Chaplin knew I was not religious and neither was Bonny. Bonny wore a white high neck dress trimmed in lace and down to floor length. She wore high heels and almost met my eyes with hers. I was dumbfounded when she entered with her mum. She was so beautiful and much more than I deserved, but then I was always putting myself down; it was the insecurity I felt inside me every day. Her dad walked beside her in his prison clothes but you could see the pride in his face. They walked up to the table where we stood, and he passed her hand to me and leaned over.

"Be good to her son." Son! That brought a tear to my eye at that moment. Son! I felt so proud that he would call me that. I saw his son's smile when he said it and I felt a wave of love then. Brian stood at least 6'2" and built like a construction worker although Graham and Billy were no different. Each were heavily tattooed and the swastika prominent on their foreheads. They looked out of place wearing suits. Her mum wore a pink taffeta dress with a fitted bodice falling out to just below the knee. She looked a little out of place with the tattoos prominent on her arms below the short sleeves. Faber was dressed in a navy blue pin stripe suit with light blue shirt and deep blue tie; very professional looking but he still looked comfortable in this tattooed company.

The Chaplin then did the usual service of marriage and then it was Jazz's turn. He smiled, gave me the rings and then hugged my leg before he moved back and grabbed Leather's hand.

"With this ring I do swear to love you, honour you in sickness and in health until death." I said to Bonny as I slipped the ring on her finger.

"With this ring I do swear to love you and honour you in sickness and in health until death." She said as she too slipped the ring on my finger.

"By the laws vested in me by the State of California, I now pronounce you husband and wife. You can now kiss the bride." I did so with gusto. I was married now with a wife, a 4 year old kid; a family and all because I was incarcerated in this prison. Maybe I owed my father a debt of gratitude after all. Leather's then shook my hand and mum kissed me.

"I could not ask for a better son in law Malcombe. She will love you son. She loves forever you know. She will wait for you to get out like I wait for my Jake, but he's not coming out now so I will have to get used to him not being around." Him not being around; For the women it is the hardest but there is always hope they will be released so they are still 'around'. Death is final and no longer 'around'. I felt sadness coming from Mable.

"Come everyone, I have a little communion wine in the chapel. Maybe we can toast the happy couple." As we arrived at the chapel which was next to the visitor hall, Cookie was there and had a couple of trays of nibbles, not much but something. We all chatted between ourselves when the 3 brothers descended on me and Bonny went off to chat with her mother.

"Good to have you in the family boss." Brian said.

"Yeah at least we know who dad wants to replace him and I know he has checked you out well and the Brothers will honour his choice."

"True Graham; I for one support you 100% and if you need help or someone bumped off, I'm your man." It was Billy. I was touched by the sentiments of the 3 of them.

"Thanks guys I have a lot to learn from your dad before I can do you all proud."

"Dad says you are ready now, you just need confidence in yourself." They all agreed.

"You 3 agreeing don't mean the whole Chapter will agree."

"They already have. A meeting was held last week to elect a new leader of the Chapter and 3 names were nominated including yours. You won hands down. That means you have absolute rule and all members of the Brotherhood will obey regardless of how they voted. When Leather's dies and that won't be too long now, you will be the boss."

"But Bonny said he had 2 years to live."

"2 years to live but maybe 6 months to know what he is doing. He has a cancerous tumour in his brain. He will become incoherent in about 6 months and unable to look after himself in about 9 months and then it will be just a matter of time."

It was getting late and the last bus went past the prison in less than 30 minutes. The guests had formalities to go through so had to leave. The chaplain then asked us to follow him and he took us to a gate where a guard was waiting for us. H unlocked the gate and we followed him through. I was still wearing the ankle cuffs so I tended to shuffle slightly. We were taken through 3 gates before we came to a small building and he unlocked the door.

"I will be back to pick you both up at 6am. Please be ready and congratulations both of you. Your case is inside Mrs. Everett and your prison clothes are waiting for you. Leave the suit on the bed when you leave." With that he walked away. I looked at Bonny then lifted her up and carried her across the threshold. We were actually alone for one whole night.

"Is there a bath?" she asked

"I doubt it; prisons don't have luxuries like baths." But I was wrong. The building had 3 bedrooms, a small kitchen and a bathroom with bath and a shower above the bath.

"I'm going to have a bath and you are going to join me my darling husband." I smiled and must have looked like a Cheshire cat with a bowl of fresh crème. "Now that's a wicked smile if ever I saw one."

"Wicked or not I am going to enjoy this bath as much as you."

Leather's had thought of everything; beauty soap, bath salts and soft towels; even a soft new sponge. For a guy in prison he had good taste and a way of making things happen. While I sorted out the bath and ran the hot water; hot water: Oh such a luxury for a prisoner. While I ran the bath Bonny appeared in a soft pink negligee and soft pink panties. I just looked at her.

"Well don't just stand there mister, get those teeth working and rip these clothes off me." She looked so inviting standing there. Having not had a woman for over 3 years and even seen a woman in her scanties for the same amount of time, I just didn't know where to start. "Come here" She said finally and I moved over to her and started to kiss her; my hands holding her scantily covered ass.

"You smell so beautiful; feel so soft and look so naughty."

"Ah now there's my tiger; lurking in the bushes but about to pounce," I couldn't get over the softness of her; the firm buttocks and full firm bust; nothing like a man felt during sex. Why did I think of sex with a man at that moment? She started to undress me; first my jacket, then my tie; my shirt buttons then my shirt was off. My belt undone and my zip lowered resulting in my pants falling to my ankles. The ankle cuffs. I looked down but they weren't there. Now I remember the guard removing them before he left. I kicked my boots off after I undid the laces and then my work socks. I was naked standing in front of my new wife: My full tattooed body in full view of this perfect woman. If I died tomorrow I would die happy.

"Why do you love me?" I asked stupidly.

"Because of whom you are and because you love me; there is a difference between the love I felt for Justin and the love I feel for you. I can't explain how or why, it just is."

"I know what you mean. My love for you grew as I felt I was becoming more accepting of myself and your own love towards me. At first I thought you loved me because your father told you to, but you didn't did you. You loved me the first time we met?"

"Did you feel that right away?"

"Yes but I didn't realise it for a few months until I realized I actually did love you."

We finally got into the bath and I washed her back in-between kissing and feeling each other's bodies; the slippery slidy wetness and soapiness of the skin after being washed all over. She noticed that my cock was ridged the entire time we were in the bath.

"Do you want to fuck me in the bath?" She asked.

"Do you want me to?" How dumb can a man be; of course she did. She leaned over and kissed me and grabbed my cock, leading it towards her pussy. I entered her easily and we held each other as I moved inside her. I kept it slow so she could enjoy it and maybe have an orgasm, but I was finding it hard to hold myself back; then she started t scream and I let myself go and we orgasmed close together.

"Did you see them?" She asked

"The stars?" I asked her

"Then you did see them. Oh Malcombe I'm so glad we married even if we only ever have this one night together." The water was getting cold now and I stepped out of the bath and grabbed a towel for Bonny. I dried her and she then dried me and I grabbed her hand and led her to the bed.

Chapter 14

Making love to a woman again was heaven. The smell of her body; the feel of her soft skin and her warm breathe on my face as she kissed me. No, I wasn't queer; I felt the passion of a man towards a woman as we fondled each other. I wished this night was somewhere else other than at the prison but that was not to be. I thought I was accepting prison life after 3 years incarceration, but the feeling I was having with Bonny made me realise what I was missing out of life. Sure Bonny was a picked bride for me but I didn't care. She accepted me for whom and what I was and I accepted her as if I had chosen her myself. I was in love with this beautiful person. I didn't care if the Brotherhood had chosen my bride for me. I would have Aryan boys with her to perpetuate the Aryan race; the Brotherhood. What her brothers had said about me being the chosen new leader of the Chapter surprised me at first but I am not against it. I'm not a racist person or at least I wasn't before I came inside this prison. Prison makes you racist to survive. The Latino's, Afro's, Ities and Mexicans, all want Leather's dead so they can take over the drug running inside the prison and also on our turf in LA and San Francisco. But I know enough now to make sure that when I take over, the status quo will remain. I know there will be battles, but I also know the Brothers here in prison and they will fight to the death.

Bonny and I lay between the course sheets and our bodies finally met. I could feel the heat of her body next to mine. She was an exquisite woman and she was my wife. Our sexual exploits lasted all night as we knew it was going to have to last about 17 years or more. We knew too that we would not meet like this ever again. The wedding night is a special night for newlyweds and although the bubbly could not be brought in, our love making that night more than made up for it. It was just braking dawn when I roused Bonny from her dream like state.

"We have to clean up and dress. The guards will be here soon to take me back and to escort you out. You were wonderful last night." I said as she wiped the sleep from her eyes.

"It was a wonderful night Malcombe; one I won't forget ever."

"I wish it could have been longer and in a more respectable place."

"It was perfect. You were here with me so how could it have been any better?"

We washed ourselves and I quickly shaved my face and head. Bonny kept kissing me while I tried to shave getting shaving crème all over her lips and nose, and she became silly and boisterous, feeling my cock and crutch while I was dressed in my prison denims.

"You look quite handsome in your denims. Mind you, I don't think much of your tailor. Dad said you had taken up foot boxing and Tai Kwando?"

"I never had to learn to fight before but in this place you have to be able to defend yourself or die. If I am to become leader of the Chapter, I have to be able to beat any of my Brothers as well as any challenger from the prison gangs. Its dog eat dog in here; so don't worry if you get a message saying I am injured; only worry about the message that tells you I am dead. Wounds heal."

"I'm used to that with dad and mum has told me that Leather's reckons you will live to see parole anyway. I'm not worried my love, so don't worry about me. I have Jazz to protect me, and even at 4 he is a real scrapper."

"Watch him Bonny. He may become too confident and become the school bully. That's not the way I would want him to grow up. Sure he has to be able to defend himself as he grows older as trailer parks don't breed lawyers and accountants; mostly unemployed and burger flippers. I want him to be proud of who he is but not become a killer like his new dad. I don't want to see him in Juvie or later in here. He's too nice a kid."

"I'll watch him but he has too many influences outside of my care. Remember he has 100 uncles at the Aryan Chapter hall." It was then that we heard a knock on the door. I went and opened it and saw there were 2 guards standing there; one with chains in his hand. I turned around with my hands in the air against the door so they could fit the belly chains, then the wrist cuffs and connect them to the belly chain. Finally the ankle cuffs were fitted and connected to the belly chain. Bonny came over when they were finished she kissed me and hugged me tight. 'I love you' she whispered in my ear as they turned me around and escorted me back to my cell block. It was a month before she was allowed back to the visiting room and I desperately missed her and Jazz.

As I entered the cell block it was ablutions time, but all saw me enter and the wolf whistles and cat calls started. Lewd remarks such as 'did you get it up' and 'did she enjoy taking it up the bum' were first followed by many others. I just smiled like a Cheshire cat and said nothing until I entered my cell. Leather's was waiting.

"Well?" He asked

"Well what?" I answered with a big smile."

"Did you get it off together?"

"I'm not queer leather's I know that now."

"Ah Bonny could always persuade a man to be a real man."

"She is a beautiful woman leather's and you should be proud."

"I wish I had been around when she hitched up with that no hoper. I'd have smashed him around a bit. She just moved in with him when she found out she was pregnant with his baby. From the first day he was violent towards her. She came to visit me with her face battered and blue. I had him beaten to a pulp; Brother of not, nobody beats up a woman in my Chapter and a pregnant one at that."

"She said you killed him."

"Me? Kill a shit like that? Not worth the effort. I got the Ities to do it for me. I told him to start selling dope on their turf. He was too stupid to know the difference. They saw him and dealt with him."

"You sure he's dead?"

"One of the boys saw him taken, then later saw them take his body down the wharf and make him part of the new wharf container pad. Yeah I'm sure he's dead."

"Bonny told Jazz I was his father."

"He needs a father Malcombe, even if he is in prison. He needs to know there is someone in here that loves him and will look after him."

"Hard to do inside here."

"That's why the Brothers are taking care of him; don't worry, he won't become a thug like his dad; new or old. He's going to be well educated and the Chapter will pay all his school fees."

"He wants to be a thug Leather's; he's even got 5 tatts now."

"Yeah Fingers did them for him but they are just small ones to make him happy. Fingers won't smother him in tatts unless he asks him when he turns 18. By then you'll be out of here and able to advise him."

Bonny always brought Jazz along since we married but 3 months after our wedding she came in beaming and Jazz was more excited than usual. As he ran up to me and jumped into my arms, he said he was going to get a brother.

"Are you pregnant?" I asked with a look of shock on my face

"Don't look so surprised; the way we went at it that night, it's surprising I'm not having triplets."

"When is the baby due?"

"First week in September they reckon."

"It's a boy dad it's a brother."

"Big mouth; you can't keep a secret can you?" Jazz went quiet for a second.

"Do you want a baby brother Jazz?" His face lit up once again.

"Yes please; I can play with him can't I dad?"

"Sure you can and help your mum look after him too."

"Can I mum?"

"Yes you can help me while your dad is in here chasing fella's."

"That's a great thing to teach a 4 year old." I said to Bonny with a smile. I knew she was just jesting.

"He's a bright kid Malcombe; don't underestimate his level of understanding. I wish he didn't sometimes but he knows what we are talking about; he asks so many questions when we leave here."

"How are you coping with me in here?"

"Good, the Brothers keep me in money as the welfare ran out. They look after everything Jazz needs and have said they will pay his school fees for a better school. I don't think he should go to a better school Mal. He needs to go to school with kids from our area so he makes friends."

"Is there more than one school near where you are?"

"No, just the one public school with a bad record: There is a private school but few from the area go to it. Jazz would need friends Mal, so he can grow up and enjoy his childhood."

"You can't pick his friends as he grows and moves through the classes. He has to pick his own and good or bad, he and we have to live with it. I just don't want to see him get in with a bad crowd and end up in Juvie that's all."

"Most of the kids in our area end up in Juvie from around 10 years old anyway Malcombe. It's where we live. Trailer parks are the lowest society in America. The kids are destined for prison. I hope Jazz doesn't end up there but I am prepared for it."

Jazz started school in the spring of that year. The Brothers made sure he had a school uniform although most of the new kids didn't; in fact most were wearing raggedy hand-me-downs from older brothers. Bonny said he was so proud of his new uniform and his new backpack for his little lunch and big lunch he had in a plastic box in the backpack. But right from the start he was having problems with school bullies from the older classes. Bonny told him not to fight back but most days he came home with a bloodied nose or grazes on his face and legs. Bonny was beside herself trying to stop Jazz from retaliating but she knew he would eventually snap. Jazz knew how to defend himself from the lessons his 'uncles' had taught him and Bonny was right to worry. She finally got the call she dreaded from the head master. She had to front up to the school and had an appointment with the principle.

"Your son beat up a child at the school today. Has he shown any troublesome behaviour prior to this?" He asked.

"No, he hasn't; but he has been coming home almost daily with bloodied noses and black and blue eyes. Don't you have teachers supervising the play areas during breaks? He is being targeted by a bully and I don't blame him for retaliating. This has been going on for several months; so don't blame him for this, blame yourselves."

"Mrs. Everett, he nearly beat the child to a pulp and he needed hospital treatment."

"Good, maybe now Justin can get on with learning instead of defending himself. If I see one more bruise on him, I will make a complaint to the education board. Mark my words Mr. Kovick; I do know members of the board."

"I'm sorry you are taking this in that way Mrs. Everett. Justin is suspended from school for 1 week as from now."

"No he isn't; he is leaving this school as of right now and I will enrol him in the Catholic School down the road. Goodbye and I suggest you find the bully before he kills someone maybe even one of your teachers." Bonny was very angry. The school didn't supervise the kids during breaks and knew nothing of who the bullies were. She rang the caretaker of the Chapter and asked to speak to Warren, Leather's 2ic for San Francisco. He came immediately on the phone.

"What's up Bonny?" He asked. "You sounded upset so Ray put you through straight away."

"Are you in a meeting Warren?"

"Nothing that can't wait: I prefer to chat to the most beautiful woman in San Francisco than these thugs anyway."

"Warren they have thrown Jazz out of school for fighting. They suspended him but I told them he's not going back. He was coming home bruised and bloodied every night and he just snapped."

"So where do you want him to go to school now?"

"St Margaret's; it is close by and maybe they have better control of the kids."

"No problems Bonny, I'll arrange for any fees to be paid and pay for the new uniform. Take him along tomorrow and he will already be enrolled."

"Thanks Warren, I don't know what I would do without you."

"How's that good looking chap of yours doing?"

"He's good Warren and as pleased as punch about the baby."

"Yeah I bet he is. Not too many men can say they've conceived a baby while in prison."

"How does Jazz get on with him?"

"Jazz knows no difference. He only knows Malcombe as his dad and they get on real well."

"I'm glad about that."

"Thanks Warren and I will take him to St Margaret's tomorrow." Bonny rang off and looked at Jazz. "I am taking you to a new school tomorrow so we better go down town and buy you a new uniform."

"Why are you taking me to a new school?"

"Because you were caught fighting; that's why."

"I beat him easy mum. He's just a bully and he hit me too much. I didn't want to hit him but he said my dad was a killer and he would never get out of jail ever."

"Well I am proud of you but I am also angry with you. They were just words Jason. They don't hurt you and you know the truth anyway. He doesn't know who your dad is and he's just mouthing off to make himself look big in the other kid's eyes. Did you really hurt him?"

"Yeah, I broke his nose with a foot slam and then broke his arm when I twisted it and then elbowed it hard."

"Jason you are 5 years old. How come you had that much strength to break his arm?"

"It's easy, Bull taught me."

"Bull? You just wait til I see him next."

"Ah mum you worry too much. I can handle myself."

"That's what worries me Jazz."

You're angry with me aren't you?"

"How can you tell?"

"You called me Jason. You never call me Jason." Bonny quickly gave him a big hug.

"You are still my favourite fella." and kissed him.

Bonny continued to bring Jazz to the prison as she felt he had to keep in constant contact with me. It was the middle of August when she and jazz turned up at the prison. She looked hot and bothered and her face was flushed. She sat down while Jazz was his usual exuberant self. We sat talking for a while and Bonny started to look pained.

"Are you ok?" I asked quickly

"Mal I think it is coming."

"What now?"

"Yes right now. Get the guard to call the prison doctor." as she said that, she slumped to the floor and I could see fluid around her.

"Guard, call Doc, she is giving birth; right now." The guard moved to the phone and rang the duty controller in the booth above us. Doc was there in 5 minutes but by that stage I already had hold of the baby's head as it emerged from the womb. Jazz just stood there fascinated as the baby was being delivered. The other visitors were held back. An ambulance was called to take Bonny and the new child; yes it was a boy; to hospital to make sure there were no complications, but the boy cried loudly as he came out and Doc didn't even have to slap his ass. We wrapped him in my white T-Shirt with California State Prison all over it. Jazz was excited he saw his brother being born and frankly I'm glad he did. It is a good experience for him. Jazz went with Bonny to the hospital but before they left, Leather's was allowed to hold him as a proud grandfather. I received a resounding roar of approval when I finally made it back to the cell block after finishing my shift in the kitchens. Leather's was as pleased as punch as he had got to see the baby.

"What are you going to call the little fella son?"

"Well I'm not calling him Leather's that's for sure. But Jake sounds good."

"How'd you find out my real name?"

"I married your daughter remember?"

"Fuck, that's right. Forgot that; Jake sounds real good to me: Jake Everett; got a good ring to it. I doubt I'll see him ever again though."

"I'm sure Bonny will make an effort to bring him on a visit when her mum comes too, then you can see both of them; Jake and Jazz."

"That would be good. I ain't got much time left son. Doctors only gave me 2 years and leaves 15 months left. Please promise me you'll keep me safe when my mind starts to go. Promise me Malcombe."

"That's the first time you've ever called me Malcombe."

"First time for everything they say."

Chapter 15

Leather's was deteriorating fast now. First he found it hard to hold things and often dropped a cup or a garden tool when working. He could no longer get his cock up and so our sex stopped but I still crawled into his bed at night and just held him. I could sometimes hear him sobbing quietly in the still of the nights. He knew he was near the end now and would never have the chance to sleep with his wife Mabel ever again. His memory was now bad and I had to start taking up the slack. When we met the bosses in the centre of the yard, Leather's would just stand there and I would do the talking. They all knew Leather's was as good as dead and the word was out I was his successor. I started to look around for a good 2ic and found one in Balls. He had been to college like me but fell foul of the law when he got caught selling drugs. He was trying to save up enough for his university courses. He wanted to do art but now he spends his spare time doing drawings on a sketch pad he had managed to buy. He got 20 years with non parole of 15 years. His lawyer didn't believe in plea bargaining.

I had finally started my university course and had passed the first and second semesters. I had to pass the last semester to be considered for outside attendance at the university. I worried about the application for outside tuition as Leather's was getting worse fast and I had all but taken over his role in the prison. He would just sit back when in the rec yard and I would go out into the centre with Balls. It was one cold windswept morning when out in the centre that the Latino head, Chico, gave an ultimatum; give up the drug running or it was all out war. I answered in saying "Try it." Chico just smirked and turned to walk away, then turned swiftly, a blade in his hand and lunged at me, but I was too fast and grabbed the blade turning it on him. It stuck deep into the ribs. I immediately turned and walked back before anyone could comprehend what had happened. The others were standing there with Chico's body slumped on the dirt. Then the sirens started and whistles and we all fell to the ground face first. We were each searched and then body searched again as we were sent inside the block. It always amazed me that they had CCTV everywhere keeping close tabs on us yet could not determine problems in the yard. I was never questioned. Once inside the questions came thick and fast from the Brotherhood. Leather's was first.

"What happened out there?"

"Chico told me outright I was passing over the drugs or it would be outright war between us. He then lunged at me with a knife. I caught hold of his hand and reversed the knife into his ribs. It was self defence but the Warden won't see it as that."

"Man he was fast Leather's." Balls said with an excited voice.

"That's his training coming into play Balls. I never doubted his abilities. Make sure you tell all the other Brothers about his speed." As he said that he collapsed and the guards called Doc. He died that night of a brain haemorrhage. As an inmate, Leathers received a burial at the prison cemetery. Mable and Bonny were allowed to attend, but nobody else, including me. They would not release the body for burial outside of the prison grounds. I was now boss; reluctant as I was. Faber came to visit me shortly afterwards to let me know that my application for the following year had been turned down by the prison board as I was classed as a gang leader and likely to offend whilst outside the prison. Faber said he would lodge an appeal and if that was turned down he would take it to the district court. I thanked him for his support.

"Why do you want to see me qualify as a lawyer Mr. Fabien?"

"Our office deals with the Public Defender's office and they have said they would be interested in having an inmate who is qualified to handle cases whilst in prison and then handle some of the gang related cases when released. You fit the bill perfectly."

"My association with the Aryan Brothers and my artistic looks aren't going to put them off is it?"

"I talked to the head of the Public Defender's office and he is aware of the tattoos and your elevation to Chapter Head but believes with legal training you will keep the Chapter on a steady path. It's not wearing the suits and cloaks that win trials Malcombe, it's knowing the law and how to read a jury that is the most important. How you look is irrelevant."

"You say that now, but when a jury sees this face my case will be lost before the charges are read out."

"Not necessarily; you can object to any jury member and basically pick your own jury. You just make sure if it's a young kid you defend, the jury is made of mothers: If it is a drug runner, then more towards men; but working class men. You can manipulate the jury without breaking the law. That is where I think you will excel."

"I want to do this degree but I might need you to help convince a few people. Have you managed to get anything on the Warden yet?"

"Enough to make sure he signs your paperwork for outside studies."

"Good."

"Did you have anything to do with Chico's murder?"

"Self defence Mr. Faber. He came at me with a knife and I deflected it into his own chest. Any CCTV footage will show that."

"Ok, I believe you."

Faber left and I was escorted back to the kitchens. I finished my duty and with the latest delivery of drugs inside me I headed back to my cell; but it was a lonely cell now. I was alone in the cell when Hairier came in.

"Got a young kid that needs training; new intake so will be up later. Make him feel at home Mal." That was the first time he had called me by my first name.

"The deal you had with Leather's still stands. You're mine now." I said like I owned him, which I did. He turned around, his face flushed with anger and I was ready for him. He tried to lash out with his baton but I swept it aside and grabbed him by the throat and pushed him up the wall. He was choking and I could see his lips turning blue. "You're mine Hairier; lock stock and corrupt. You will continue the deal you had with Leather's only now it's with me; you got that? I own your ass." All he could do is try to nod. I let go and he slid to the floor. He got up from the floor and sat on my bed for a few moments until he could compose himself.

"Will Balls still be paying me?"

"No, I haven't decided who yet, but you'll find out at the end of the month. Just keep looking away."

"Why did you kill Chico?"

"Who said I did? I never touched him."

"I saw the CCTV footage before anyone else did. You owe me for destroying that footage."

"Then you would have seen him flash the blade. Self defence is a powerful defence Hairier. No jury would convict on that footage. Make sure I get a copy of it tomorrow and destroy the original."

"I can't destroy the original; the Warden has it locked up."

"Then we will have to unlock the safe and get it out. I will let you know when and expect you to have the area safe for us."

He walked out rubbing his neck. I could see my finger marks as red blotches still showing. I wasn't sure if he had decided to stay with us or just playing along. I would watch him closely. The new kid arrived after lights out again, and I could hear him sobbing as they closed the doors and he heard the locks engage.

"Don't worry about making the bed in the dark kid. Jump up here and cuddle up." I had moved to the upper bunk after Leather's passed away.

"I'm not gay. I'll sleep here thanks." I jumped down, grabbed him and slapped his face hard.

"I said jump up here and cuddle up. You do as I say from now on, I'm your new Chapter leader kid and you ain't got any choice about it." He picked himself off the floor and came at me. It was hard to see where exactly I was but my eyes had already adjusted to the dark and I managed to duck his punch and then smashed his head into the metal supports of the bed.

"What you do that for?" He asked

"You don't answer back fuckhead. You are my fuckhead and my pussy from now on; you got that?"

"Fuck off you queer." I then smashed him with my fist and laid him flat. I left him there overnight. He was still there when I awoke. His face was bleeding bad and his eyes swollen from my fist. I didn't let up. Once I got off the bed, I pulled his head up level with my cock and made him suck me off. His cheeks were wet while I face fucked him.

"It don't have to be like this kid. You got no choice. I fuck you and you suck me off. You accept your place in this cell and we'll get on real fine."

"Why? You're just a queer fuck." Again my fist struck home, his nose was bleeding and face swollen; eyes could hardly be seen out of.

"Make your bed fuckhead and do it properly. Bed inspection is in 15 minutes and you got to be shaved and have a shit before inspection too. You better move quickly." I then sat on the toilet and he looked at me then moved quickly to make his bed and shave. I made sure I took as much time as I wanted on the toilet as I knew I could shave quickly and in time. He was a blonde haired blue eyed beauty, about 18 year's old maybe 19; not well built but promising. A few tattoos and he would fit in just fine. He was mine to do as I wanted. "What you in for Fuckhead?"

"My name is Collin." He said. Again my fist found his face.

"Your name is Fuckhead now while you're in prison kid; get used to it."

"Why you doing this; I done nothing to you?"

"You got to learn Fuckhead; learn how to survive. You're my fuckhead in here and my Brothers know it. You're an Aryan Brother now. Training starts today. So what you get caught for?"

"Drugs; got 20 years with 15 years non-parole. It was just party drugs not heavy drugs. I got caught with the stuff on me at a night club in town. I tried selling it to an undercover cop."

"Your first mistake kid; selling to those you don't know. Second mistake is being blonde haired and blue eyed. Kiss your good looks goodbye. You're a member of the Aryan Brotherhood now and you better learn to fight and to kill on demand."

"You mean I got to get tattooed like you?"

"Yeah and you'll get to like it kid or die. We don't have anything in between. You got a girlfriend?"

"No; a few female friends but no girlfriend."

"Well now you have a boyfriend so get it through your head you are now a queer, like it or not." I had to be brutal otherwise I wouldn't be able to train him to do my job in the kitchens and deliver the drugs.

Fuckheads first day was in the kitchens washing the large pots and pans. I could see his disgust on his face as if he was above this type of job.

"Get used to it Fuckhead, you're in prison now kid and you ain't worth a bag of dog shit. You eat what they tell you, sleep when they tell you, dress how they want you and work where they want you for the next 20 years; and don't get your hopes up about parole either. It's more likely you will get more years added to your sentence as you become institutionalised and start to rebel. The Brothers will protect you all they can but you've got to be protective of yourself to survive in here."

"I just want to get out of here; I don't belong in here." He said almost crying.

"You committed a crime Fuckhead and got caught. You belong in here just as much as I do and everyone else does in here. You're a criminal just like us and your life doesn't mean shit in here. Upset anyone and you're as dead as meat. Being young you get to be fucked and to suck guys off. As you get older the roles might change. Either way you'll be as queer as anyone inside these walls when you get out."

"You got a girlfriend?"

"I'm married and 2 kids."

"Then why do you fuck guys?"

"Ain't no women in here kid, just men so if I want to get my rocks off, your ass is just fine for me."

"Doesn't your wife get disgusted knowing you fuck men?"

"No she knew before we got married. Her father was a con so she knew the score."

"Why do I have to be a kitchen hand? Why can't I do something better?"

"Because you're my fuckhead and you got to run the drugs from the kitchen up to the cell. Cookie knows the score and will give you the drugs each day."

"But the guards search you at every door?"

"Not up your ass kid and down your throat."

"What I got to swallow them and shove them up my ass?"

"Easy when you get used to it. I did it for 5 years. You'll get used to it, won't he Cookie?"

"Piece of cake kid; Nobodies ever been caught neither." We finished our stint in the kitchen then Cookie showed up to where the stash was and I downed my share and shoved the large one up my ass. Then it was Fuckheads turn. He

105

found it hard to swallow the condom until I shoved it in his mouth hard and it slid down. I then pushed the string down and he nearly choked. Then the ass; His ass had not been conditioned before like mine had, even if it had only been a couple of days. Fuckhead was a newbie and first day in jail. I pulled his pants down, got some grease and smeared his ass then rammed my cock up it. I thought his eyes would fall out of their sockets I worked his ass for a while then pulled out and quickly shoved the condom up inside him. It slid in easy with the string pocking out. I then shoved the string inside him and pulled his pants up. He was now my courier as well as my fuck relief. I had no problems converting over from a bum boy to the rapist; it was a natural progression.

Faber tried his hardest to get my application for outside learning approved but the prison board still refused to budge. He finally took the matter to the court of appeal and won. He also let the Warden know he had a few things to show the appeals board but the Warden finally signed the release form and the application was approved by appeal. I was to travel each day in the prison bus to the university and back each night. A prison guard would accompany me into the lecture halls and I was not allowed to talk to anyone and had to sit separated from the rest of the students. I was the only outside student at that time from the prison and had to wear my prison uniform and remain shackled at all times.

3 Weeks into my semester and the prison was in lockdown. The Latino's and Ities had a pitch battle in the rec yard. My boys stayed out of it for as long as they could until it spilled over then the Afro's and the Aryans become involved. 3 prisoners were killed in the riot and I reckoned they had been the original targets and the riot was just a front to cover up the kills. It was 4 days before we were allowed out into the rec yard again and being a Sunday, I

was at the prison. I walked out to the centre with Balls and the other bosses sauntered over with their own protectors.

"Why the riot Renaldo?"

"We had some vengeance to attend to and a riot was the best way."

"Why didn't you clear it with the bosses first: We would have sorted out the problems and saved the riot."

"I doubt you would have agreed to these kills. They were paedophiles and sex offenders. They had to go; my guys didn't want to be near them."

"None of us like those guys but why not ask us first so we are aware and can cover you?"

"One of them was your new guy; the one sharing the bed with Stars. Sorry Scar, he had to go."

"I saw he was on the list of dead: Didn't put 2 and 2 together. Ok, no revenge killings you got that?"

"We're done killing. You have our word no revenge killings."

"While I'm out at University, Balls and Gruber are my mouth piece. What they say comes from me, ok?"

"Why Gruber? Since you beat him up he has the mentality of an earth worm." Renaldo said smiling.

"Yes agreed but a very faithful earth worm and very skilful too. Don't underestimate his loyalty to me."

"What after you nearly beat him to death?"

"Even after that, his intelligence level now doesn't allow him to think too hard and he only sees me as the boss. He doesn't remember the fight at all."

"Ok, but Balls is a strong fuck and I'd hate to come up against him in a dark alley."

"He's more than a match for you Renaldo so remember that and he has a brain on him too; a dangerous combination in this place."

"When are you passing the drug trade over to us Scar?"

"In your dreams Renaldo; you have more chance of a pardon than taking the drugs off of me."

"Maybe the next riot will have to answer that problem."

"You try another riot and it will be your life that is in danger. My boys are ready for you anytime. We have no beef with you and your gang Renaldo but you start to target my boys again and we will all but wipe your gang from the face of this earth. That is a promise I will keep."

"You certainly have a way with words college boy. Don't threaten me or my boys or we might just take you up on the offer of a full out fight."

"Today ok or do you need time to plan your attack?" I threw a glance at Balls and Balls made a gesture towards the gang. They immediately went onto alert. It was then Renaldo made the first move again; the other gang members had also seen the gesture and had made sure their boys were also ready. Renaldo slashed at me and this time Balls was ready for him. As soon as Balls moved the Aryan's raced into the fray along with all the other gang members. It was a pitched battle within a few minutes and Renaldo was dead before the others moved. The sirens started to wail, the whistles sounded but the fight continued. The boys all wanted to make their marks. My boys targeted the Latino's and they made a hefty impact on their numbers. It wasn't until the guards started to shoot into the fray that we quickly lay flat out on our faces and waited. The guards then came round to each individual and lifted us up and patted us down, checked the ground around us then moved us back into the block. As I moved back into the block I noticed 3 of my boys injured but 8 of the Latino's lying motionless.

8 Latino's died that day and not one shiv used. My boys were expert at using what they had natural and that was sheer strength and they were all found with broken necks, Renaldo included. The Afro's had helped and so had the Ities. They hated the new Latino boss as much as we did and wanted him dead. Although the bosses of the Afros and Ities didn't like the Aryans, they did not try and take the drugs off of us as we had the system all tied up. We had the means to get it in and to distribute it. To try and take it over, they knew they would need to work a new system and that took time and money before they sold the first gram.

Chapter 16

Fuckhead had to be tattooed and blooded. There was a new intake of crims that day and word throughout the prison was there was a sex offender coming in. This guy bordered on psychotic having killed 3 girls; raping all 3 and cutting their genitals. Fuckhead would have to kill this slime as his blood in blood out. Balls would make sure he did it while I was at uni. Needles already had a go at him last night and the Swastika had been done, the spider's web on his right elbow and giant SS lightning bolts with 88 on his back. On each side of his neck, Needles had already tattooed the Shamrock with the triple 6 and the head of Himmler on the other side with the 'Deaths head of the SS underneath. He was looking more Aryan by the day. His handsome face was fast disappearing under black ink. I had to slap him around a bit as he walked with his head down in shame about the tattooed look. He had to learn to walk with arrogance, up straight to produce fear in those who saw him. He had learnt to force the dugs up his rectum and down his throat and was not objecting to the sex at night or sucking me off first up in the morning. He was starting to accept his lot in life inside prison. Prison changed a man and when a man first enters prison he is scared but time takes this fear and replaces it with confidence especially when an Aryan Brother. Fuckhead would learn to be an Aryan Brother, learn to fight without fear and build his body up to be in the peak of health and fitness. Balls' was his fight instructor and Grub his body building instructor. Needles would continue to cover his body in tattoos and maybe one day he would be as proud of his tattoos as the rest of the guys. He was aware that to be an Aryan came with a real awareness of power and control. The Aryan Brotherhood ran the prison but not just this Prison, every prison in the USA.

I had continued to send semen to Bonny so she could transplant it into herself; for more than 2 years after our baby was born and it finally bore results. Bonny became pregnant again and she beamed as she entered the visiting area with Jack now walking, and Jazz the proud big brother. This time Jazz didn't tell me.

"You look like you've got a secret you want to tell me Bonny"

"I'm pregnant again and I think it might be with twins."

"Twins? Fuck how you going to fit 5 of you into that trailer?"

"It will be hard but they are your kids Malcombe and I don't care how squeezed it is. There is a larger van in the trailer park up for rent with 4 bedrooms but it is expensive."

"Go to the Chapter and see what they can do." I looked at Jazz and saw a tattoo on his arm. "Fingers been at you again Jazz. Those tattoos are becoming noticeable now. Have to curb the tattoos boy before they start to get you into fights."

"Already have dad, but I haven't lost a fight yet."

"I don't want you fighting Jazz; it will get you into Juvie and I don't want that for you."

"I am an Aryan Brother. Prison and crime is what we are."

"Jazz you are 10 years old and still a boy. To be an Aryan Brother you have to kill someone. That could be life behind bars kid and that is not the life I want for you."

"Already killed a guy for Sparks in the Chapter: The guy didn't pay for his drugs and used the drug money from sales he made: I just walked up to him and stabbed him in the alley. No problems dad. Nobody saw me." I looked at Bonny and saw the horror on her face then I looked at Jazz. His face was cool, calm and collected.

"How can we stop what is happening Bonny. He's 10 years old and already blooded in to the Aryans. This can't be happening."

"We can't get away from it Malcombe. Once blooded in you are blooded out and that's death; you are in for life."

"Fuck I never wanted this to happen. I never wanted to be an Aryan myself but had no choice. Jazz was already part of the Aryan's before we met and married. Leather's saw to that. I'm sorry Bonny I never wanted Jazz to be so involved."

"I don't think either of us had a choice. It was in our destiny. Jazz was the grandson of a Chapter Leader and had to be blooded in, even at an early age. It was his destiny as will be prison. We can't stop it Malcombe."

"I'm starting to realize that Bonny. It will happen to Jake and the twins and any other children we have. They are born into the Aryan Brotherhood. It worries me but I have to accept it as the life of an Aryan leader."

"I am the wife of an Aryan Leader and I know what is required of me and my children. My father knew this and that's why he wanted me to marry you. I don't regret it Malcombe."

"Neither do I Bonny. I love you very much; I just want to get out of here and live with you and the kids and live a normal life. It will happen one day but I still have 13 years before I can apply for parole."

"You will get it Malcombe, I know it."

"When are the twins due?"

"June next year; I will try and work it as close as possible so I have the birth here at the prison if I can."

"I may not be so lucky this time. They may not let you in so close to your due date."

"I'll be there dad, I'll help her."

"I know you will Jazz but only if you stop getting in trouble and stay out of Juvie. Please kid, stay away from the Chapter house."

"I can't dad; it is part of my life."

They left and I was again shackled and led back to the cell block. As a leader of a gang I was shackled everywhere I went; checked bodily before entering the block and generally feared by the guards. The Aryan Brotherhood has been known to escape their chains and kill guards. They can secrete a key to cuffs up inside their nasal passage then release it and unlock their cuffs. This has happened twice in San Quentin and the guards are very wary of escorting Brotherhood members. The guards killed were brutal thugs themselves and had to go. We despatched them; one with 38 stab wounds before the Brother was subdued, but the job had been done. The other died of stab wounds along with two other guards who were seriously injured. Both these guards had caused problems for the Brotherhood and had to be dealt with. The Brotherhood members knew they had to kill when told and also knew they could be killed themselves. Justice is swift when the Brotherhood is involved. Those who are found guilty of killing a guard know they face Lethal Injection and they accept this. We all accept this as our whole life is dedicated to making sure the Aryan Brotherhood remains the main force inside prisons and outside on the streets.

I was now into my third year of studies and passing well. I received a visit from the head of the public defender's office, Michael Deveraux; and we talked for quite a while in an interview room.

"Do you want to join us at the public defender's office Malcombe?" He asked.

"If you really want a tattooed freak as a lawyer then yes I want to join you."

"It's the fact that you are tattooed and a leader of a gang that we want you to take on cases inside this prison. The prisoners you will deal with will respect you more. You will not be allowed to represent you client in the court but there is a new way through computer software, and we can actually have you do your court defence through Video. We have agreement from the Chief Prosecutor for you to use this facility and it will be run through a separate channel direct to the court. The feed will not go through the prison system and as such be private."

"When do you expect me to start?"

"When you complete your third year, you have to work with a lawyers firm to study further. As you are in prison that would normally be unobtainable for you, however as a Public Defender and using the video system, we can overcome this."

"I would love to become a Public Defender."

"Fine, I will start the paperwork and let you know the outcome." He then left and I was again shackled and led back to my cell block.

Life in Prison never changes. As Leader of the Aryan Brotherhood, I had to discuss problems with the Brothers; about problems with other gang members, other gangs and also the drugs and condone killings. I was fully institutionalised now and accepted prison for what it was; brutal and unforgiving. I decided who would die to protect our gang and to make sure our gang remained the dominant force in the prison. Most of the time we are the smallest number but we are the most aggressive and therefore the most feared. We run the drugs and are the leading gang in the meetings of gang leaders. What we say goes and we take no crap. Chico and Renaldo died because they became cocky and tried to take over; the Latino's have not tried again since. However, there is a new gang trying to make their mark now; the Mexican Mafia. Styled on the Italian Mafia they are almost as aggressive as the Aryan Brotherhood so we have to keep them in check and killings are the only way. The boys are instructed to kill any Mexican Mafia member they find in a vulnerable position. In January 2008, 3 Mex were killed in separate actions; one in the rec yard and two in the shower blocks. One Brother was finally charged over the yard killing and is held in Solitary pending court appearance. It's not expected his appearance in court will be before the end of the year.

Trial dates are not important for prisoners as they are already locked up and under guard. I am hoping to be his defender. I was finding it hard to pass my 3rd year semester exams as finding peace and solitude to study was almost impossible at the prison as my duties as leader always came first.

My final semester exams and I was as nervous as hell. Bonny had tried to get her birth of the twins in the prison but the prison authorities had refused visiting rights for the last 3 months of her pregnancy. The twins were born on June 12th 2008 and both boys: Twins yes but not identical. They were easily identifiable as different. Both were blonde and blue eyed but each had a different facial look mostly the nose. One had my nose the other Bonny's nose. One was bigger than the other and would more likely be taller and thicker. When Bonny finally was allowed into the visiting room again, Jazz carried the newborns his latest tattoo showing grandly and his beaming smile as he carried both boys with ease and in each arm. Bonny held Jake's arm and he was a bundle of energy.

"Why the new Tattoo Jazz?"

"My birthday present from Finger's: I love it."

"The swastika emblazoned in such a large tattoo on your lower arm is not a good idea Jazz; you are going to have to fight more often with this one. The Jews also have gangs kid and they will target you now."

"Already had a run in with the Jews and won, injured a couple badly too."

"You are becoming a dangerous kid. You're next home will be prison Jazz. Remember, it ain't like home, and others will target you if they feel threatened."

"I'm prepared for that dad. The Brotherhood said they want me to start a Chapter in Juvie. I want that dad; I want to be active in the Brotherhood. It's all I know."

"I understand Jazz but it is not the life your mother or I want for you. We want you to be better educated and have a career. Maybe follow in my steps and become a lawyer."

"I'd rather dig ditches or sweep roads than go to University. No I know prison is where I will end up so please don't try and talk me out of it dad."

"How can you decide that at 10 years old Jazz; you don't know your own mind yet?"

"I know enough to understand what I have to do for the Brotherhood. The brotherhood is my life dad just like you. It will be Jack's life and the twins life too so you can't stop it even as a leader. Get used to it dad."

"He's right Malcombe, you don't have any control of him and his mind is made up. I don't discourage him as I know he is totally into the Brotherhood. His mind is totally absorbed in the lifestyle. Nothing I say makes any difference to him. It's like a drug he can't get off."

"He is too young Bonny. His life will be ruined before it even starts."

"The police already have an eye on him. I don't expect him to stay out of jail for too much longer." As she said that I saw Jazz smile.

"Good, the quicker I am inside the quicker I can do the work of the Brotherhood for them." He was lost to me and I saw it there and then. If I had been outside and able to control him, maybe I could stop this but he was determined to do time at Juvie. I couldn't stop it. It was 2 months later when he was arrested for the murder of a member of the Jewish gang. I wept in my cell that night. He was now part of the criminal element of this city and would only live in hell from that day forward. Even at 10 years old, he had built up the hatred and aggression and love of the Brotherhood. He was an Aryan Brother even at 10 years old. I was forced into it but he went willingly head first into a life of death and destruction. Bonny now had to divide her visiting time between us both.

Chapter 17

I passed my year 3 semester exams. I was not outstanding barely getting a pass mark. But the head of the public defender office was happy at the pass grade and organised for me to get clients at the prison. He would pass information to the Warden and the warden would arrange for the prisoner to meet with me in an interview room. I was given the same privileges as a normal lawyer and could request the video and audio be turned off. My first case was a young black prisoner who was trying to appeal his sentence. He had committed armed robbery and sentenced to 25 years with 20 years non-parole. It was a harsh sentence for a first offence but it was also well known some judges would sentence the black youth to harsh prison terms as they were biased against black youth. I looked over all the evidence sent to me and when I interviewed him asked why he refused to tell detectives the names of the other guys who carried out the robbery with him. He had been the only one identified from a CCTV camera at the scene. No weapon was found on him and none seen on him in the CCTV film. Had he just been in the wrong place at the wrong time or had he really gone there to rob the joint. I asked for the entire tape to be sent to me in Prison and it was agreed and held in the warden's office for my viewing. I checked it out thoroughly and noticed a guy behind the fixtures of the fruit department of the store and maximising the frame I saw it was my client. He was shopping and as he walked to the counter, the robbers entered and he saw it was friends from his neighbourhood. He was as shocked to see them there as they were to see him. They passed a knife to him and he threw it away but that was all that was needed for the court to find him guilty. I had to convince them he was not part of the planned robbery but just an innocent bystander. I prepared my defence and got the video section where my client could be seen shopping blown up by the Public Defender's Office and the scene where he was given the knife and he threw it away. I was nervous on my first day in front of the camera but a phone call from the head of the Public Defender's Office helped cool them down.

I laid my case and called on the prosecutor to study the new evidence and to allow the appeal to be up held. I also asked that the youth be given compensation and assisted to find work. The case lasted for about 4 hours before the Court of Appeal adjourned for lunch. After lunch both the prosecutor and I had to address the bench. But I was ready and the warden had agreed to have food sent to the interview room for us both. When the bench came back, the prosecutor spoke first and I nearly fell off my chair.

"Your Honour's, it is obvious my department was lacking in its duty and did not have this matter fully investigated. This office fully agrees with my learned college that a gross miscarriage of justice has occurred and we offer our apologies to the defendant. We recommend release immediately and all charges expunged from the system."

"Council for the defence; Do you want to add to this statement from the prosecuting office?"

"Yes your Honour. My client has been imprisoned for over 12 months and institutionalised in behaviour and thinking. I request he been given assistance to return to a normal lifestyle and for your Honours to determine a suitable amount for recompense for his imprisonment and denial of his basic human rights. I have studied this personally and determined a figure of $50,000 which will allow him a chance to settle into a community and maybe buy a small home of his own. Plus I request the social Services assist in finding my client work to match his mental abilities and he not be burdened with parole officers and his address and records be expunged from the judicial system. He needs to be left alone and not harassed by police. He is married and has a young son so he has a chance to stay out of prison in future."

"You put your case well Councillor. I award the defendant $50,000 by the Prosecutor's office and $50.000 from the SF Police department. These amounts will be paid within 30 days. A Parole officer will be appointed to the defendant but his brief will be to find work for the youth and not as a parole officer. I will brief him personally. On behalf of the court of Appeal: I apologise for the mistakes that have happened to you. Courts sentence based on evidence given in court and not on what might lay behind it: However when a mistake is made, the Court of Appeal must make restitution to a wrongly sentenced defendant. Enjoy your life and you are to be released within 24 hours." My client just looked at me and broke down. I held him close and let the sobs calm.

"You are free Gregory and when the paperwork comes through later today, you will walk out of here a free man with no criminal record. Go home to your wife and be happy but stay out of trouble."

"Thank you so much I never thought I would be free again."

"Why didn't you tell the investigating police about what actually happened?"

"I would have had to name the guys and I am not a snitch. To snitch is to die in my neighbourhood."

"You will have enough to buy a small house in the suburbs Gregory so get out of the gang areas and live where your child can grow up free."

"I will. Why are you doing this? You are an Aryan Brother yet you helped me; a black?"

"That is now my job and you were no threat to me or my gang. Black or white, my job is to defend to the best of my abilities." I called the guard's in. "This man is a free man as from 30 minutes ago. Take him back to his cell so he can collect what he wants, protect him with your lives and then take him to the Warden's office. Oh, when he gets there, make him a coffee or tea. He is no longer under your control but as free as a bird. He won his appeal." The guard looked at me then smiled.

"I think you have become more dangerous now than ever before Scar. A brain and the most lethal mind are hard to beat in a prison. I have been meaning to talk to you about that Mexican killed last week out in the yard. I'm sure you know nothing about it."

"If I did Sir, you would be the first I would tell. Then I'd have to kill you, so feel safe in the fact we have not talked recently."

"You wouldn't kill me Scar; you'd get one of your boys to do it."

"I never shirk my responsibilities. If I have to kill I will without remorse. Of course you would find it hard to pin it on me." I was then shackled and moved back to the cell block. I was barely there when I was called out, shackled once again and taken to the Warden's office. Gregory was sitting there dressed in civilian clothes and his wife had arrived and sat with him with their baby son.

"I wanted to thank you for what you did for Gregory, Scar. It will be a new life for us."

"Keep him out of trouble. He knows the hell of prison now and that should keep him out. Be happy and get away from the neighbourhoods and gangs and have a happy life in the suburbs."

"We will and thanks again."

"Take him back." The Warden shouted. I could see he was not happy. The Warden was still on our 'to kill' list and we were ready anytime to do the deed.

We finally had the opportunity to kill him later that year during the fall. He had inspected the cell block with guards and then entered the toilet alone. One of the Brothers saw this and moved forward towards the toilet. The others saw what was happening and started a fight in the cell block rec area. They ripped the chairs and tables from their mounts and threw them at the guards and then the siren opened up and guards came from everywhere, but the deed was done; the Warden was dead and not a sight of blood anywhere. Snake had just snapped his neck and sauntered back into the rec area and joined in the fight. The CCTV cameras did not catch the intruder nor his exit as the fight was around the entrance to the toilets. The Prison was in lockdown for 4 days afterwards and the Brotherhood interviewed separately more than once but the same story was told and no charges were laid. The new warden came from a softer prison from down south and we had no problems with him. He was black and surrounded himself with a few new black guards but always put white guards in our cell block.

To qualify as a full lawyer, I had to do a year as a clerk with a firm of lawyers, however being in prison made it hard for me to qualify in that regard. I received dispensation from the Californian Legal Commission to carry out my legal clerical position as a public defender from prison. My boss, the head of the Public Defender's Office, came each week to see me with new briefs and information. I had usually 3 to 4 clients each month; most for Parole hearings but a few appeals. Gregory was the only appeal I won but then he had been innocent. The others I had no doubt they were guilty and although I was their lawyer, I found no grounds for a lesser sentence. However I did manage to have the non-parole periods lowered and they were happy. One of the clients, a Mexican, later died from stab wounds inflicted by the Afro group after he had stabbed one of their men. The Mexicans became one of the most hated groups in prison. The Aryan's were the most feared but the Mexicans hated for their attitude and vicious actions against other gang members. Even their own members were not safe. Their leader was a psychotic killer and felt all his men should kill all other gang members every time they were in the outside rec area. There was never a time you could discuss problems with him. It was decided by the other leaders he had to die. It occurred in the outside rec area while he was in the weight training cage. Two guys held him down while Balls dropped a 200 lb weighted bar on his head and it rolled onto his neck and throat. He suffocated to death before help was found. Nobody was ever charged and as for the warden and guards, it was a relief he was dead. The Mexican Mafia knew who had killed their leader and we all knew it would come to a head soon.

It was 2 weeks after the death when the first signs of trouble reared its ugly head. Once again the rec yard was where the riot started and the Aryan Brotherhood was deliberately attacked. The Afro's and Ities stayed out of the fray, but surrounded the main fights to mask the CCTV. In containing the fights it was to the benefit of the Aryan Brothers. We had always trained our men and close combat was our forte. 4 Mexicans died that day, but no Aryans, although we did have some serious injuries to 5 men. The rest of the guys had minor injuries and easily fixed by Doc. I received several stab wounds but mostly on my arms and legs and no torso wounds so a few stitches fixed me up. I was interviewed by the Warden and I swore the Mexican's had attacked and we had defended ourselves.

"You left them with 4 dead Scar."

"Did you notice not one was stabbed? Whereas my men were stabbed, so where are your own men's skills in searching the Mexican's cells? Your men are falling down on the job Warden. My men can fight and taught to fight with their bare hands. We don't need shivs and metal to fight. Knives and shivs have to be hidden and easily found but your own training and strength cannot be stopped. My men can kill with their bare hands Warden and leave no evidence."

"So that's how you killed the previous Warden?"

"You said that Warden not me. We have no beef with you Warden and your life is safe with us. We will protect your life with our lives. You have my promise."

"I'm not sure if to thank you or cringe at that Scar. You are a cunning man and a brilliant mind. Leader of the Brotherhood is a dangerous position in this prison. So far you have done nothing that would cause me to send you to another prison and to be honest; I would prefer you here and your control of the Aryan Brotherhood rather than have a new leader to have to get to know."

"Better the devil you know than the psycho you don't."

"Why did you pick to join the Brotherhood Scar? From your records you had no previously recorded contact with them?"

"I didn't choose to join but once a part of the Brotherhood I relished it with a passion. My wife was involved, my father-in-law was a Chapter leader and my son is now a member. My family is the brotherhood Warden." The Warden then signalled to the guards to take me back.

Chapter 18

I was called back to the Warden's office about a week later. I was to be sent to Juvenile Hall to defend a young Aryan Brotherhood member who had been charged with Murder: A Justin Herguard.; Jazz. It was his arraignment later that week and I was instructed to defend him. I would stay for the entire trial at Juvie in a special room. It was solitary confinement but I was allowed special privileges to allow me to defend Jazz. The Warden of the Juvie was not aware of my association with Jazz. Neither did the Public Defender's Office. My last name was Everett and jazz had never agreed to the name change when I married his mother. To see jazz in shackles being dragged into the interview room made my heart bleed. But he had a big smile on his face.

"I told you I would do the Brotherhoods' work in Juvie dad."

"Yes you did but you didn't expect the shackles and loss of freedom did you?"

"Yes I did and I feel wonderful dad. I am now just like you and granddad. I am a prisoner and will serve my life in prison. Like father like son. I am happy dad, happier than you can imagine." I saw then he had planned this murder and had wanted to be imprisoned since a child. Now I had to defend him and my job was to try and get him off. The last thing I wanted was for him to be sentenced to life; to serve part of that sentence in Juvie then the remainder in an adult prison. I knew he was a tough kid and trained by the Chapter to take their word to Juvie. He had been picked and trained to be a murderer and end up here. Jazz had been blooded in; his life now was for the Brotherhood and no other. Even if a miracle happened and I managed to get him off or a reduced sentence he would still remain a criminal as he would be in and out of prison the rest of his life as a member of the Brotherhood.

"I want you to tell me exactly what happened the night the guy died."

"I was at home with mum, Jake and the twins. It was about 10 pm when I heard glass breaking. I checked it out and found a rock had been thrown through the front door window. I raced outside and saw 4 guys standing across the road. I went inside, grabbed a knife I always kept in my jacket near the door, told mum to stay inside, and then went out to meet up with them. They were members of the Jewish gang and started to jeer me on saying I was helpless when I was without my Brothers. I lost it and when the fighting stopped and they left, one was bleeding badly and they were dragging him. I don't know where I stabbed him as I think I stabbed all of them somehow."

"So you fought them all; all four of them?"

"Yes."

"And how old were they?"

"In their twenties I think."

"The fact that you faced them with a knife does not fare well but the fact that there were four and in their twenties against a 10 year old boy should go in your favour." He became angry then and stood up but the fact he was shackled and the chain attached to a floor ring meant he was not able to move from his seat.

"I killed him: I want to go to Prison. You can't stop me going to prison Scar, you just can't."

"Jazz my job is to try and stop you going to prison or find a way to reduce your sentence. I know deep in your heart you want to serve the Brotherhood but you are 10 years old Jazz. I really don't think you understand the realities that go along with prison. Once you enter prison, even Juvie, you will never be the same man. Your sexual life as you grow up will be with men and it depends on who is stronger and more violent as to whether you get fucked or you fuck the other guy. It's not all fighting for the Brotherhood Jazz which is what I think you believe. No, I will fight to keep you out of prison for as long as I can. I realise I might be fighting a losing battle and you will end up in Prison eventually but I hope by then you will know life a little more." I saw he was holding back tears, trying not to look week in my eyes.

"You have to let me go to Prison dad. It is where I belong like you. I have been trained to start the Chapter in Juvie and now I have the chance. Please don't stop me now."

"The information I have shows the man who died was 23 years old but there is no mention of anyone else in the report or being injured. The report alleges you stabbed the man on the street in back of a shop alleyway. They said you chased him to the shop and stabbed him there."

"That's not true. I stabbed him outside home. His mates dragged him there and left him to die."

"Which means they are as guilty as you: If they had called the ambulance immediately their friend was stabbed he might be still alive now. By moving him they could have caused irreparable harm. That is almost as bad as killing him themselves. I will ask my boss to try and track down the other 3 men. How did the police come to talk to you about the killing?"

"I followed the men to the alley but they dropped the body and ran through the alley to the other end when they saw me. The police arrived quickly after they left and I was found over the body."

"Did you tell them about the attack outside your home?"

"No, I didn't tell them anything. It was my chance to go to prison and I wanted to go there so I said nothing until you asked me questions."

"I will have to get someone to try and find those others who attacked you and soon. I need to know if they were stabbed. It's our best hope of getting you off or a reduced sentence."

"Why dad? I want to go to prison."

"I don't want you to go to prison for something you didn't do Jazz. It's hard enough to do time for what you did let alone for a crime you didn't do. Please let me decide how to defend you Jazz. With your mindset you will enter prison with or without my help; I just want you to be older and more able to handle it when you eventually do go to Prison. You are so determined to go to Prison Jazz; it's like a disease with you."

"It's what I was born for dad. It's what I am trained for. I can fight well; I know how to use a knife and my bare hands. My muscles are getting bigger and I know how to keep strong and develop bigger muscles. The Brotherhood has trained me for this dad."

"I know Jazz, but they have broken the creed and have interfered with a Brothers family. They were supposed to support you all not to train you. That is a violation of our creed and I will deal with that separately from within."

"What you going to have Snake and Finger's killed for teaching me?"

"Would that worry you?"

"Yes, they are my friends."

"But the creed says if you fuck up then the Brotherhood can end your life so why does it worry you? You say you are a Brother so if I decide to kill them for breaking the creed and ask you to kill them, then you are duty bound to carry out the execution as directed by your leader."

"Please dad, don't ask me to kill them; they are my friends."

"Then you can no longer be a member of the Aryan Brotherhood and I have you killed instead then have them killed too. To be a member of the Aryan Brotherhood you must obey without question Jazz. This is no game for kids. This is deadly serious. So, will you kill Snake and Finger's for me?"

"I don't know if I could do that dad."

"Then I must kill you instead. I will not do the kill myself but I will have another prisoner or a corrupt guard do it for me. Keep looking over your shoulder son." I could see the eyes were wet now and I hoped my being direct would throw him off a bit. He was 10 years old and his thoughts were too old for his years. I had to scare him hard. To tell him he had to kill a fellow Brother and a friend would be the hardest thing he would have to do in his life.

"Please don't tell me to kill them; please?"

"Then you have to let me defend you and get you out of prison. This is not the time for you to enter into a life in prison Jazz. Please let me defend you as I see is best?"

"Please don't ruin this for me dad. I want to go to prison and I need to be in prison. I killed that man and I need to pay for that."

"I will defend you with everything I have jazz and if I can get you released then I will. It will not be against your desires as an Aryan youth to be released. I'm sure you can start your own Chapter here in Juvie before I get you released. You will not have failed son."

My request to the Public Defender's Office to have the other men investigated immediately did give results. The other 3 men were tracked down and sure enough, they had cuts and marks on their bodies. There was a CCTV camera close to the entrance to the alleyway and I was sent a copy. It clearly showed the body being moved into the alleyway by the 3 men. The body was lifeless at that time. It then showed Jazz entering and then the police shortly afterwards. The police had said they had found a knife in Jazz's hand when he was found. The knife was similar to the wounds found on the body. Now it was my turn to find a defence for jazz. I requested the 3 men as witnesses and also the senior officer at the scene. I also requested Bonny as a witness. The arraignment was to be by video and we sat in the interview room. The prosecution laid its case and then after lunch, It was my turn. They had called only two witnesses, the police officer who had made the arrest and the pathologist who had examined the body. It was now my turn to call witnesses and Bonny was first. She confirmed the rock thrown through the front door and that Jazz had gone out to confront them. She also said they were just standing there and did not move when Jazz had gone out to meet them. I then stated to the judge that they had provoked the attack and Bonny agreed.

The 3 other attackers were there in court as they had been arrested for tampering with a body and were to face court later that week. I questioned each and one was obviously the leader of the pack so I concentrated on him.

"You were all in your early 20's?"

"Yes."

"And yet you provoked a 10 year old boy into violent action?"

"He came out of the house with a knife."

"Would you have done the same faced with 4 men twice your age?"

"Maybe but we didn't."

"No you stood like cowards waiting for a 10 year old boy to exit the house and come after you."

"We are not cowards."

"Then why attack the house of a 10 year old boy?"

"He was in the Aryan Brotherhood."

"So that gave you the right to take the law into your own Hands? He was 10 years old for god's sake. He was just a boy."

"He had attacked Jewish boys at the school he went to. My son was one of those he attacked."

"So you reported it to the principle of the school?"

"No, we decided to teach the boy a lesson ourselves."

"A vigilante group against a 10 year old boy: You should be ashamed of yourselves."

"He is Aryan Brotherhood and stands for everything we oppose. They are racist and against the Jewish faith."

"So you took the law into your own hands?"

"Yes."

"And the man who died as a result; he was alive when you carried him from the site of the stabbing."

"Yes but he died soon afterwards."

"So you dumped his body in the alleyway and just ran?"

"When did you call the police?"

"When we saw the boy enter the alleyway."

"So you set him up for the fall when by moving your friend you actually killed him. If you had called the ambulance straight away, you might have saved him. That boy was protecting his family as he was the only male in that house. Of course he would have come out to meet you; he isn't a coward like the 4 of you were."

I then questioned the other two me and basically got the same answers. The court was then adjourned for the day. It would be resumed the following day at 10 am. I received a call from my boss at the Public Defender's Office.

"I was at the court Malcombe and was impressed. You have the prosecution running to catch up. They rang me a few minutes ago to suggest I meet with them for a plea bargain. What do you suggest?"

"Total exoneration for Justin: It was self defence and against overwhelming odds. I will ask the Judge to dismiss the charges on this basis."

"I think you will get it. I will talk to the prosecutor's office." He rang off and I knew then Jazz would go free but I also knew it would not be long before I was defending him again. Jazz was angry when I told him what had happened.

"I told you I wanted you to keep me here dad. You failed me."

"No I didn't fail you jazz, I saved you from a lesson you should not have to learn so young. I am sure you will end up in prison soon and I won't be able to help you then but I hope you will understand your own mind better and be able to handle it easier. Prison is not just another home Jazz. It is a place where predators lurk and you being young regardless of if you can fight well, you will become someone's bitch and get fucked every day and night. I don't want that for you jazz."

"I can handle myself."

"Can you? Can you fight a 200 lb muscled man and stop him beating you up the forcing you to suck his cock or from fucking your ass? Your body has many years before it will develop a man's body Jazz and before it can develop muscles to be able to be on an equal footing with these men. If you end up in Juvie for a serious crime, you will then be transferred to an adult prison when 17 or 18 years old. You will have no chance Jazz and end up some guys bum boy whether you want it or not. You're not a queer Jazz but you will be in prison."

"So? I take what comes. You had to and look at you now."

"I was lucky and leather's took me under his wing. You might not be so lucky and end up with some queer queen and unable to get out of it. There are plenty of them even in the Brotherhood. You cannot guarantee being placed in the cell block of the Brothers either. Each guard is aligned with some gang or other and you'll end up where they want you not where you want to go."

"I'll take my chances."

"You're just stupid and boneheaded Jazz, maybe I should leave you here to rot." I saw a smile on his face and I hit him hard with the back of my hand. It stunned him at first, and then the look of hate came over him.

"You're just as much a coward as those guys that attacked my home."

"No Jazz I'm your father and I'm just trying to make sure you have a life, not live in an institution."

The court resumed the next morning and the prosecutor stood to give his address. He demanded that jazz be given the highest possible sentence for a juvenile. He stated that the murder was premeditated as jazz had exited the house armed with a knife. His speech almost swayed me into thinking Jazz should get the maximum sentence, but then it was my turn.

"Your Honour, my client did exit his home armed as the Constitution allows for all to bare arms. He was provoked into defending his mother and brothers; all unable to defend themselves. For a 10 year old boy to willingly face 4 adults is a courageous act and not of a killer; he was defending his home as allowed by the Constitution of the Country. The fact that he injured one of the men was in self defence and should not be a chargeable offence. The men who were there that night killed their own friend by moving him from the scene. The fact that my client followed them was to make sure they were well away from his home. The other men dumped their friend's body in an alleyway and on seeing the boy enter, then rang 911 and reported the killing. They ran like cowards and left the boy to take the rap. They are now in custody on a charge of moving a body from a crime scene and my client must be released as the charge of murder must be downgraded to self defence. I rest my case and rely on your learned council for review of this case." The judge adjourned the case to the following morning for a decision.

The case was the first on the day's agenda. Jazz was called to stand even though he was in front of a video.

"You are charged with First Degree Murder. I find the charge not substantiated by council for the Prosecution. I do however find that your actions; although courageous; were ill advised and stupid. I sentence you to 3 months incarceration to be served at the juvenile detention centre but with time already served you are to be released within 7 days once the final paperwork is finalised. I hope to never see you again in this court for to do so, you will be dealt with harshly. This court is adjourned." Jazz looked at me and I saw his hatred in his eyes.

"You freed me when I asked you not to. I hate you."

"You were not guilty of murder Jazz and the court saw that. I didn't free you, you did that yourself. You are still a criminal in the eyes of the law and the Brothers won't think less of you. I'm sure that in your state of mind you won't stay out of prison long." Jazz turned and left the room. I was right; within one week of his release he had killed another Jewish man only this time it was a random act and could not be considered self defence. I asked not to defend him and this time he was sentenced to life. I had failed him. He had to serve 6 years in Juvie but would be transferred to an adult prison at age 16 years. He was lost to Bonny and I and would become the thug he wanted to be and I doubted he would live more than a few years before he was himself killed.

Chapter 19

I continued to act as defence council for those thought too violent or at risk of escape to be taken to the court for appearance. I handled their cases through the medium of the videotaping from the prison. In that first year I defended 7 prisoners and received plea bargains for only 2. Even that was a miracle as the evidence on both was quite open and shut but the method of collecting the evidence was in question so the prosecutor was willing to do a deal to gain a conviction. Faber kept in contact with me regularly and on a visit on my 7th year after conviction, he appeared more excited than usual.

"I think I have some new evidence in your case Malcombe. I am still checking the investigation but I believe it might be significant."

"I pleaded guilty Faber; there is no appeal for me."

"Appeal no, but a retrial yes."

"But I killed those people as sure as I plunged a knife into them."

"Did you? Something kept niggling at the back of my mind. You said you had drunk 10 drinks that night over a 6 hour period. Your blood alcohol level was not consistent with that amount. It was more consistent of between 15 to 20 drinks and that amount would have either killed you or left you totally comatose. I don't think you were driving that car at all."

"But the police said I was the driver?"

"I checked out the original report from the first police on the scene and from the paramedics. I don't believe you were the driver."

"You mean I have done nearly 7 years in prison for nothing?"

"Possibly but I still need more evidence. I need to be absolutely sure of the evidence before I take it to a court."

"If the evidence was rigged against me, then who had it... My father; but why?"

"I believe he saw problems with the insurance on the deaths. In my investigations the policy on the car was not registered until the day after the accident. It was registered by a local company in your home town. Your father was registered as the owner of the car. Police reports showed it was reported stolen later that day. The insurance company never paid out a cent on that accident. Your father was a lawyer for a company that represented that insurance company. As I said, there is a long way to go before I can take it to a court."

"I don't understand why my father threw me to the dogs? We always got on so well."

"You became a threat and an embarrassment to his standing as a corporate lawyer. I'm also sure the corporation he worked for leaned on him greatly to do what he did. Again investigations are ongoing."

"My life is already ruined Faber. Why try to help me now?"

"You have gone through a lot Malcombe and if these allegations are true then you have done time illegally and I intend to right that wrong."

"I can never be anything other than a member of the Aryan Brotherhood now Faber. Why don't you just leave things alone and let me rot in hell. I have already destroyed my son's life; how many others do I have to ruin?"

"We are both lawyers Malcombe and we will always seek justice. You knew your son was headed for a life in prison but you still fought for him and won, but his freedom was short lived. You did what you thought was right and I will always do the same. I advised you to take a plea bargain based on the evidence presented to me but the evidence was corrupt. Neither the prosecutor nor I were to know it had been tampered with. You have paid dearly for that tampering and now someone has to pay and pay they will."

"Promise me Faber, you will not request compensation. I don't want compensation as I have no way to use it. My family will live on what I earn when I am finally released and nothing more."

"Why Malcombe, it will allow you to get away from the Brotherhood and live an easier life. You won't have to ever work again."

"I am a member of the Aryan Brotherhood; blooded in. There is no leaving the Brotherhood alive, Faber: Blood in; Blood out."

"I could arrange for you to live in a Federally protected program well away from San Francisco."

"No, I don't want that and I'm sure Bonny doesn't either. San Francisco is Bonny's home and the Brotherhood as much of a family as she has ever had. I know Jazz was corrupted by the Brotherhood but I assure you Jack and the twins will not have any contact with them if I can help it."

"You have to be out of prison to do that Malcombe. I will let you know how the investigations are going when I am in SF again."

"Leave me be Faber. Let me serve out my sentence and live in peace."

But Faber did not leave it alone and his investigations were discrete but thorough. He even managed to find a copy of the CCTV of when we all entered the car on our way home, and CCTV footage of the actual accident and arrival of police and paramedics. He brought them with him to the prison on his next visit. We sat in the Warden's office to view the evidence and there it was. I was drunk but one of the others in the group got into the driver's seat and I entered the back and sat in the centre seat. The accident was not caused by alcohol either; or at least not by the driver of my car. The car was hit from behind by another car and forced into the barrier then careered across the 4 lanes into a light pole and another car. All but I were thrown out of the car. I had to be cut from the seat of the car where my legs had been wedged against the front seats and my chest crushed by the seat belt. I had been the only occupant of the car wearing a seat belt. Faber managed to have the footage checked and the license plate of the car that hit my car identified. That car had left the scene before police had arrived. Police were now questioning him about the accident.

"Your father had been contacted about the accident but was not told that you were not the driver; he assumed that being your car you would have driven it. He then contacted his friend at the insurance company and had the insurance details changed. A friend at the DMV also changed the details of the registered owner. Both these people are now in police custody. It was his friend at the DMV that suggested he report the car stolen."

"So I didn't kill my friends and neither did the driver of my car? I have lived with that for 7 years Faber. 7 years of guilt. I put up with prison life and the Brotherhood because I felt the guilt of their deaths. I deserved everything that happened to me. But I am a thug now Faber as much a thug as any in here. I am a criminal as much as they are.

Prison does that to a man. I am as much an animal as they are, and my life now is as institutionalised as they are. I don't even know how to shit by myself without being ordered to do so. How am I going to live outside with a wife and 3 kids? I am just an animal now; a killer in my own right. Don't let me get out Faber, for heaven's sake don't get me released."

"You're just scared now you have realised you might actually have a chance of getting out. I can't stop fighting for you Malcombe; it's my duty as your lawyer; anyway, you know you have a job to come out to as a lawyer with the Public Defender's Office in San Francisco."

"I won't take it Faber. It is fine while in prison but not outside. The Brotherhood has many businesses outside and I will be given a job by them. I don't want to be part of the law ever again."

"But why Malcombe? You are a good lawyer."

"Maybe but I was stitched up by corrupt lawyers and corrupt police. I don't want to be part of that. How can I be sure that evidence given to me is accurate. Look at what happened with Jazz. They never even looked into the evidence but just took what they saw as fact. No I don't want any part of that."

"I'm sorry Malcombe I have to follow this through. It will not be a short process and may take several years to get permission for a retrial. In your present frame of mind I'm sure that won't worry you." Faber then stood up and left, showing his anger at my reluctance to ask for a retrial.

Chapter 20

I could not get it out of my mind that I had served 7 years in prison for a crime I had not committed. The knowledge that I had killed 5 people allowed me to accept Prison and its harsh discipline. To now know it was all a mistake left a bad taste in my mouth and I was angry with the world for allowing it to happen to me. My life had been all planned out; University, joining a law firm, getting married and having kids, buying a house in the suburbs; a dog, maybe two and a nice car. Then wham: My life was just stopped in mid air. I awoke in a prison cell, covered in plaster and strapped down, taken hundreds of miles away from my home and put into a prison hospital then when recovered, into a prison cell with animals. I had to become an animal to survive. I am an animal to this day; willing to kill to keep my status in this hell hole. I rape young men new to the prison system; not because I need to relieve myself but to show my strength to them and my men in the Brotherhood. I had to maintain a leader's status. My 'bitch' was the drug runner for the Brotherhood; my cock sucker, my boy pussy. I was the leader by appointment not by vote. I had married the leader's daughter before his death so became his natural heir. I allowed the Brotherhood to tattoo me so I took the form of a Brother; allowed them to torture my mind with their teachings and culture. But I was an Aryan Brother; I accepted their teachings and culture; I accepted their racism and killings as necessary to maintain our dominance of the prison. I had now killed 5 men inside the prison and felt no remorse. Two had been leaders in their own right; Reggie had been a necessary blooding for my entry into the Brotherhood. The other two were deaths required by the Brotherhood requested from the San Francisco Chapter for acts against the Chapter at some time in the past. One had tried to leave the Brotherhood and that was a death sentence; the other had attacked a

Brother and killed him. Until he was sentenced to life in prison, he had been kept in protective custody, but he was now in an open prison environment. As the leader of the Chapter in the prison, it was my duty to carry out the execution: I did.

I had two choices left me by Faber. Remain in prison or allow the retrial. I could derail Faber's request for a retrial by confessing to the 5 murders and allowing myself to be tried and sentenced, then I would be out of the reach of Faber's plan as I would be sentenced to life 5 times and no chance of ever being released from prison, and to be honest this was my best choice; a choice that would not scare me anymore. I knew I could survive life in prison but could I survive life outside of prison? I was scared to leave prison now after 7 years. I didn't know how I would react to being free; if my mind would allow me to be the family man I wanted to be. Would the violent side of me come out when with Bonny? I knew I was now a violent man; I was no longer a sweet innocent youth. I was a convicted criminal with violent tendencies. If I got into an argument with Bonny, would I become violent and strike out maybe injuring her or worse kill her? Could I be a father to Jack and the twins Michael and Andrew? Could I make love to Bonny like I had the day we married or would I dream of men while fucking her? In fact could I even try to make love to her after 7 years of male sex? Questions, questions and more questions: My mind was in turmoil with so many questions. I requested to make a phone call to my wife. I had only ever requested a phone call to Bonny on her birthday before but I had to talk to her. I was allowed 5 minutes only; hardly enough time to even say hello as she would have so much to say or tell me. The phone rang and after a short time she answered.

"Hello?" She answered

"Bonny, it's me love, sorry to ring without notice."

"Is there anything wrong?"

"Wrong no but I have to ask you a question."

"I'm listening."

"You know what I am now and what I have become. You know how the prison changes a man in here. Can you honestly say you want me to live with you and help bring up our children knowing what I am?"

"That's a deep question Malcombe but I don't have to think about it. Yes I want you with me and yes I want you to help raise our children. Jazz still needs us both Malcombe so please when you are out you still have to be a father to him. Your father abandoned you but you must not abandon Jazz. He needs you more now than ever, an ex con or not. One day he will be released and he will need us both to help him come to terms with normality."

"There might be a chance I can be out in a couple of years but I will explain when you next visit."

"I was going to visit Jazz this weekend and I am scheduled to visit you the following week."

"I don't know how you put up with us both. You never miss a visiting day for either of us do you?"

"It's because I love you both as a wife and a mother. It doesn't matter what a child does Malcombe they are still your children and you will love them to the end."

"Try and get there early for visiting day. We need to talk. I love you, bye."

"I love you too Malcombe." I then rang off. I decided there and then I would not oppose Faber's attempt for a retrial.

My life continued as normal, well as normal as prison life allowed. I enjoyed my daily work outside in the prison gardens, although the winters were cold but invigorating. I had a prison denim jacket which cut the winds but held little warmth. Fingerless gloves allowed me to work the soil and use simple garden tools. Being a leader, I was allowed to work mostly unguarded and I enjoyed this little bit of freedom, imagining I was working in my own garden at home. Home: Where was home? It wasn't in San Francisco; it was in Los Angeles but I had been denied my home by my father. I would now live in San Francisco with my wife and 3 children; but where? Bonny lived in a small trailer in a trailer park on the outskirts of SF. Could 4 of us live in a small trailer without killing each other?

My whole life was a 9 by 6 prison cell with a steel door at one end and a solid concrete wall with a minute window high up on the other. I lived with my 'bitch' who shared my single bunk and kept me warm on cold nights; sucked me off each morning and was raped by me each night before we slept. I had ordered this innocent youth to kill a man before I allowed him to enter my bed and defaced him with racist tattoos on his face and body. I had made him learn the creed of the Brotherhood and adhere to its every word. In 12 months he had become as dangerous as I was and had been disowned by his family for his gang associations. His fight training had been easier for him than it was for me as he had been more into sports and was fitter. His body was benefitting from the weight training and his chest, arms and legs expanding. He would be a big and well muscled man later, a true Aryan Brother. He had objected to the creed and culture at first but as it was beaten into him he accepted it more and more and finally he became a true member of the Brotherhood. In the 12 months he had been in prison I had seen him change from a rebellious youth to a dangerous criminal; tattooed over his entire body including his entire head. He had one redeeming feat none of us could carry out; that was being able to swallow a shiv totally and then regurgitate it as required without injuring himself. He had found it easier than I did to swallow the condoms of drugs too, although the condom inside his rectum was still difficult for him.

Faber reported back regularly about his investigations but he said it was slow progress. Each time he requested information, he would receive only a quarter or half of what he had wanted and had to request more which always took time, but he said he was getting close.

"I'm thinking of confessing to the 5 murders I have committed inside the prison." I blurted out on one of his visits. Faber looked at me with horror.

"You what? Why? What will you achieve by that?"

"To remain here in prison."

"Why do you want to remain in prison? You were never supposed to be here in the first place Malcombe."

"Wasn't I? Maybe life decided this is where I should be and I don't want to challenge life."

'I can understand you might feel hesitant."

"Hesitant? More like sheer terror Faber. Do you understand what you are asking me to do? I am already institutionalised and that normally means that an institutionalised convict will reoffend and end up back in prison. I don't think Bonny could take that. I am better remaining in prison than to be released only to end up back here with a life sentence 3 months later."

"You're quite definite aren't you? You would confess to those killings just to remain in prison?"

"Yes."

"Malcombe, the trial of one of the men involved with your father's cover up is due for trial in 3 weeks. The other is due in 3 months. There is one other, the policeman who is being investigated and is expected to be charged shortly. His trial may be 6 to 12 months away. I have to wait for verdicts on all three before I can request a retrial based on those results; if they are found guilty. The sentences will allow me to have the guilty plea overturned on the grounds that the evidence submitted to the prosecutor and to the defence lawyer was corrupt and did not allow a full view of all evidence to allow the question of going to trial or asking for a plea bargain to be properly decided. The fact that they had now found and charged the driver of the other car now meant the trial of the Culpable Homicide charges would take a further 2 years at least, so I was going to remain in prison for at least 2 to 3 years more.

"What am I going to do outside Faber? It will be close to 10 years of prison before I have any chance of a retrial. 10 years of being locked up; I don't know if I can have a normal life after that."

"I've told you that there is a job waiting for you Malcombe. You will be a free man with no convictions against your name. You will be a lawyer with the Public Defender's Office (PDO) and respected. There are many lawyers who are tattooed although maybe not on their faces and entire body like you, but tattoos are being accepted more in the legal profession. I honestly believe the tattoos will be to your benefit when dealing with young gang members. The head of the Public Defender's Office says he really needs you to handle the many gang members coming through the office. They don't relate to the normal lawyers and with your body art, he believes they will see someone more on their side and able to understand their lives and their poverty better. Most of the youths have grown up in the slums of the city; gangs have been part of their lives since they could speak. Most never went to school or left at an early age knowing there was more money to be earned in crime than working for it. You will look as much a part of their lives; the gang look they are more used to. Give it a chance Malcombe. These youths need you more than you know."

"I see these youths come in here Faber. Their attitudes are of a kid ready to fight the world. They are angry and blame society for everything that has happened to them. Then prison gets them. They are raped, beaten and abused, yet they accept it as part of their lives' as if this is what they expected and what they have already been part of out on the streets. These kids are already lost to the world, so how do you expect me to turn them around and make good citizens out of them?"

"I didn't say you had to change them Malcombe. Your job is to make them feel someone cares what happens to them. Your job will be to get the best possible outcome for them. There will be some you can't help but then the prison will deal with them. You can only try."

"I get too emotionally involved Faber and that's not good."

"You don't think I didn't get emotionally involved with your case? I'm still emotionally involved. I never thought you were guilty but there was nothing in the way of evidence for me to change the outcome; but I never gave up Malcombe and now I know you were not guilty. The driver of the car that rammed you and killed your friends and left you injured inside that car will be charged with their deaths. I don't think he will get a plea bargain."

"Make sure you tell me his name and make sure he is sent to this prison. He will make a great 'bitch' for my men, maybe a gang whore."

"Revenge is sweet Malcombe but I doubt your men will have the chance."

"We are in every prison in this country Faber. We have long tentacles. He will be one of us soon. He will suffer what I suffered; he will feel the pain of rape, the pain of being tattooed on every piece of skin on his body. He will feel the pain of institutionalising. He will know what I went through and more. My Brothers will make sure of that."

"Killing him will not solve anything Malcombe."

"Who said killing? I said he will feel what I went through but he will feel it until the end of his days. I want to stay in prison until he is in my hands Faber. I want to be the first to rape him, and have him suck my cock. I want every Brother to rape him on his first night in prison. I want his face tattooed so heavily the first night that he will wish he had stopped his car that night and owned up to his crime. Kill him? No, I will torture his mind as mine was tortured. He will become an Aryan Brother and be forgotten by his family. He will become just a number on a criminal record as I was only with no chance of reprieve."

"I have already talked to the prosecutor on the charges to be laid on him. He will be charged with murder on 5 counts as he failed to stop after the accident. With all the other charges of failing to stop after an accident, culpable driving and driving in a manner likely to cause death or injury, his sentence is likely to be around 160 years. There will be no non parole period set as a charge of murder does not allow for parole in his lifetime."

"Why murder and not manslaughter like my charges?"

"He left the scene of the accident and did not report it to police. In the 7 years after the accident he made no effort to notify police. Therefore the charge is murder not manslaughter."

"If I decide to go along with your retrial, when do you hope for that to occur?"

"Not until there is a verdict in the murder trial of the other driver. That could be 2 or 3 years away. I'm sorry Malcombe but your freedom is not close. Murder trials are notoriously slow coming to court."

"Don't worry Faber; I ain't going anywhere soon anyway."

After he left, I was called into the warden's office. He had received a file from the PDO and they wanted me to defend this guy. When I looked at the brief, I nearly threw up. It was for the guy who had driven the car that had hit my car that night on the freeway. I looked at the Warden and shook my head.

"No way Warden; this is the guy that put me in here. I can't be impartial on this case."

"I have a letter for you from the head of the PDO." He gave it to me. I read it and then looked at him then passed it over to him to read. It read:-

Malcombe'

I understand this case might seem more of a joke to you instead of a serious brief, but I truly believe you are the best person to defend this client. You will understand when you meet him. He is being sent to San Quentin on remand and I have arranged with the State Prosecutor for his trial to be held in Los Angeles and for you to represent him in person in court. Faber has contacted me concerning your possible retrial and I believe this trial will establish you on the legal lists of Los Angeles and with this office. Please consider taking this case, even if only as a personal favour to me.

Karle Howritz

Director in Charge

Office of the Public Defender.

"You are to meet the defendant tomorrow when he arrives from Los Angeles. I have been asked to place him in your cell block instead of the remand cell. I have not received his files yet but they should arrive by courier before he arrives about 6 pm."

"I will make sure he has a cell mate to look after him."

"I am having a CCTV camera set up in that cell so don't think of doing anything stupid." I was then taken back to my cell block with the files that had been sent to the Warden; again shackled. I was used to the shackles now and expected it for all movements as a leader of the Aryan Brotherhood. I would read the file cover to cover before the lights were turned off.

Chapter 21

I didn't like what I read in the brief. He was a gang member and had been to prison previously on a stabbing charge and got 9 years with parole after 5 years. He had been released just 4 days prior to the accident and although jailed, his driving licence was still current. From that piece of information alone, I deducted that his driving skill would have been impaired through lack of having driven for the previous 5 years. Was this an excuse for what he did? Would a court see this as an excuse for his poor handling of a car and take it into account? But he had left the scene of the accident without attempting to assist those injured in the accident. There was no excuse for that; but an explanation of being on parole at the time and not wanting to be put back in prison. He had been 24 at the time of the accident so had been 19 years old when first jailed.

His gang association was with a drug dealer in Los Angeles. Drugs usually ended up with a life sentence but he was not charged on any drug felonies. He had been charged with stabbing another gang member in a 'Turf' fight in Western Los Angeles. His name was suspicious; I had no photo of him but the name sent shivers down my spine. Odawa Brown didn't sound white to me. It sounded Black. Fuck; Fuck; Fuck. The boys were really going to like this guy. Somehow I had to keep him alive and represent him in court and this time face to face with a judge and jury. I would not, however, keep him safe from rape and bodily injury. I could not stop that here. He had been to prison before so he knew the game. I don't think he realises where he is to be housed during his remand. His Afro Brothers will try to have him sent to their cell block. I have to talk with the leader of the Afro gang.

Directly after breakfast was our outside rec period; I walked into the centre of the quadrangle alone this time, and waited for the other leaders to join me. I waited until all leaders were present.

"As you are all aware, I have taken on briefs for the Public Defender's Office since qualifying with a law degree. Those briefs are sent to me and I have no choice as to whom I defend. Today I have a young black man arriving at the prison and I have been asked to defend him. He will be housed in Cell Block H with my gang. I will demand my Brothers leave him totally alone and safe. It is unusual for the Aryan Brotherhood to swear an oath for safe passage of a non Aryan in their cellblock, but in this case we will. He is a gang member from LA and they felt I would be better suited to his defence. I can't say more than that but I ask you all to bare with me and leave this prisoner totally free from harassment."

"I need to talk to him and make sure he knows he has a gang inside this prison to defend him should he need help from Aryan's." It was the Afro leader.

"No, he is not to have any contact with your gang. I am trying to defend him in a court of law and I need his full cooperation. For him to associate with the Afro gang at this time may be detrimental to his case. I'm sure you want his case to be as hassle free as possible, and looking at his brief I know I can help him."

"He won't last 24 hours in your cellblock Scar. You know that and I know that so why lie to us."

"I will guarantee his safety. Should anything happen to him by any one of my boys then I will walk out into the centre of this quadrangle alone and let you do what you must. This I promise. Mind you the usual sexual rape and 'Bitch' duties are not included in that guarantee. He will be treated like any normal new prisoner in that regard."

"If I see one mark on him Scar, I will demand your life. I make that promise to you."

"And you shall have it." I walked back to the main area where the Brothers stood. We would be all together later that afternoon before the guy arrives. I will lay down the law to them then.

I finished my work in the vegetable garden, washed up and headed for the cellblock. While outside I was unchained but as soon as I entered the building, I was searched and shackled and moved back to the cellblock. I wore the denims whilst outside but when in the cellblock I had to redress into the orange smock and pants. We all had to look the same. I called my Brothers together and told them what was going to happen that night.

"Grub, this guy will be your new cell mate." Grub or Gruber was the Brother I had attacked and I had beaten him so badly it had affected his mental capacity. He had never held it against me although his mental capacity was now much diminished and he viewed me as a living god now.

His body was still muscular and strong as he was made to continue to work out, and although diminished in his mind, in a fight he was nimble, devastating and fearless. Grub would look after the new man, black or white, with his life if need be if I tell him he is his responsibility.

"Scar this is against the creed and culture of the Brotherhood. A black man is never allowed to cross into our cellblock. He is entering our turf." This was Balls speaking and he was my 2ic.

"We allow others to cross into our turf if it is required Balls. This is necessary for us to show the other gangs we can be respected to carry out our word. This man has been sent to me to defend. I can't defend him if he is dead. It is all of your responsibilities to make sure he is protected from your fellow Brother and from the rival gangs. When out in the rec area you will surround him and keep him safe. Should something happen in the outside rec area or anywhere inside the prison, you will get him to safety immediately, even if it is your life you sacrifice. If even a scratch is seen on this guy, then I must walk out into that quadrangle alone and unprotected and allow the Afro gang to kill me without reprisal. Do you all understand?" There were murmurs of unrest and I could see they didn't all agree. "Grub you have to keep him safe and defend him if attacked."

"Can we still fuck him and get him to suck us off?" Snake looked like he wanted to bash someone's head in. I could see the anger in him and knew if there would be any dissention it would come from him.

"I wouldn't expect anything else Snake. I'm sure you will all make him welcome and relieve yourselves at the same time. But be warned; no rough stuff and no bruises. This guy is to be treated with kid gloves. I have a personal interest in the outcome of his trial." The mood changed somewhat when I said they could welcome him in the traditional way, but he would not be blooded in, nor tattooed until I said so. "Needles you will stay away from him until I tell you different, that understood?"

'Ah boss when can I give him a signature he'll never forget?"

"Soon: When I decide and not before."

He arrived around 8 pm that night and as I suspected he was black. He was taken to Grub's cell but I was waiting for him. He looked at me in horror; knowing where he had been housed and I could smell the fear emanating from him. Fear has its own smell; distinctive and unmistakable. I told him to sit down and to listen.

"You know where you are Brown. You've been in prison before and you know the routine. You will get fucked and made to suck the guys off, but you expect that don't you? What you don't know is that as from this day forward, you will be fully protected by the Aryan Brotherhood as decreed by me. I am the leader and what I say goes. If a hair on your head is harmed by any one of my Brothers, he will die. You don't know why do you? I hope you never do." With that I walked out but as I exited, I turned. "I have not protected you from my Brothers on the sexual side so don't think you will not be raped. They have an open brief on that. We will talk again tomorrow and if you are not aware, I am your defence lawyer. That's why you're here and not in a cell by yourself in the remand section."

"Why you goin to defend me? You're an Aryan Brother and against blacks."

"As a lawyer and a Public Defender I don't chose my clients. I would prefer not to have to defend you but I have no choice and I assure you I will defend you the best way I know how. You don't deserve it but it is my duty." Gruber then walked in.

"This the guy who hit your car Scar? He got you 70 years in here. I don't know why you want to defend him?"

"Enough Grub, he doesn't need to know that."

"Did they charge you with the murders of those guys killed in the accident?" I looked at him in disgust and walked out.

"You better not cross him kid; he will kill you sure as look at you."

"How can he defend me when I put him in here?"

"He knows that by defending you he will be released from here eventually and he could not live with himself if he didn't defend you with every ounce of his breathe. He is a killer Brown but he is fair and the best leader this gang has ever had."

"You admire him don't you?"

"He beat me up very badly but I deserved it. Yes I admire him."

I requested an interview with him for the following morning after breakfast. We were given the interview room and this time I was not shackled and neither was he. I had asked for the video to be left on as well as the audio. I wanted a copy made available to study later. I needed to watch the way he held his hands, the eyes and his body movements to determine whether he was telling the truth or lying to me. I had the video and audio recorded every time we used the interview room.

"Grub let it out of the bag last night. I'm the guy who took the fall for your actions and had his life ruined; because of your refusal to own up to the accident. I have been asked to handle your defence and I will do so. You will get the best defence I can give you as a lawyer, and I will not be refused any assistance I need to manage your defence.

What you tell me here is of the strictest confidence and goes no further so I need you to be brutally honest with me. I am aware that some of the facts will hurt me and I might become angry inside but I assure you I will act in your own best interests and not mine. Why was I assigned to you? You are a gang member and I am a lawyer and also a gang member and leader of the Aryan's inside this prison. It is important for a defence attorney to understand the workings of the mind of his client. Most don't understand gang members, but I do and that's why you are here in San Quentin and not LA; why I am defending you and not some ponce in a suit. Do you object to me representing you?"

"Yes but I doubt the Public Defender's Office would change my lawyer. I hate everything you stand for Scar; everything."

"I don't hate blacks Brown but I would prefer you were back in Africa where you belong but that's not going to get you a proper defence. You are stuck with me now and together we have to make this thing work; like it or not."

"Prefer not." I then got up and walked to the door and knocked. The guard opened the door.

"Take him back to his cell and throw him to the lions." I said in a disgusted manner. The guard then shackled him and led him away. "Mind what you wish for Brown."

The Brothers were not comfortable with Brown in their midst and I could see him sitting well away from the guys during periods in the rec room. Grub always sat with him like a protective lion protecting her cub. I know he felt unsafe; you could see that by the way he was constantly alert; ready to pounce at a moment's notice. The Brothers were doing as requested and leaving him alone. They made no effort to include him in anything. He was finally given a job in the kitchen as a dish washer and Fuckhead and Brown had to work together. Cookie made Brown run drugs back to the cellblock with Fuckhead. This gave us an increase of drugs to sell inside the prison and became quite lucrative while Brown was on remand. It took several weeks before Brown felt more accepting of me as his lawyer. I made sure we met on a weekly basis and gradually piece by piece I managed to drag the truth from him. I felt no pity for him as he knew what he had done but his own self preservation had stopped him owning up. He knew he had allowed someone to be charged and sentenced to prison for his acts yet felt no remorse. He actually laughed when he said it and I felt like killing him there and then, but held my temper; but only just.

His fear of returning to prison was real. He had been someone's 'bitch' and when released from prison found he could not relate to women and started to seek out men. He was disgusted with himself and started to find ways to harm himself but seldom went through with it. His old drug boss found him and made him start working again and he got into several fights. He hated what he was doing and hated what was happening and when the accident happened he had tried to drink himself into oblivion but still got behind the wheel of the car his drug boss had given him to deliver drugs to the street guys. He couldn't handle being out of prison yet when he had the accident; he drove away for fear of losing his parole. He didn't want to go back to prison but he knew at least he was safe there. If he was taken by a strong man in prison he knew he would be protected and have the small luxuries these men could give him to make prison more bearable.

"When did you start to drive after being released?"

"It was the day of the accident. The drug boss had seen me that day at my sister's house. I had been sent to a half way house close to my sister and in the area I had been brought up in. It was also the gang area of the gang I was associated with in Prison, the Afro 13. As I left my sister's and walked down the street, his goons grabbed me and threw me into a van and tied me up. They took me to the Boss of Afro 13."

"Why didn't you tell the parole officer when you got back to the half way house?"

"I never went back there after they abducted me. They gave me the car and told me to deliver the drugs and gave me a list of the places to deliver. They said my sister and her family would be killed if I didn't cooperate."

"What happened after the accident?"

"The car was badly damaged but I could still drive it; just. The boss was mad as hell and beat me up. He had his goons take me down to a warehouse I don't know where, and they beat me up, breaking my nose and also my right arm. They held me there for over a week before they let me go and the gang doctor fixed my arm."

"The gang doctor?"

"Yeah, they had a doctor who had been struck off for drug abuse and they plied him with drugs and he looked after the gang injuries including gunshot wounds."

"So how did you remain under the police radar for so long? Your car and its registration plates were quite visible on the CCTV from the freeway?"

"Boss had plenty of police in his pocket; he had to if he was selling drugs. Corrupt cops are dime a dozen in LA."

"So where did you live for 7 years while I was doing time for your misdemeanours?"

"Boss owned several warehouses and each had an underground safe house. You entered them from an industrial area away from the warehouse and went through a tunnel and came up inside the safe house. There was no entrance from the warehouse. They were safe and even the police on his payroll didn't know how to enter. He also stored drugs there and we were allowed to have drugs when not working."

"Were you under the influence of drugs when the accident happened?"

"I'd been given an injection of Heroin when I was grabbed. The boss kept his couriers Heroin dependant so they didn't rat on him and always willing to work: No work, no Heroin."

"So you are a Heroin dependant?"

"Yeah and I ain't had it for months now. I am starting to feel better but I still get the jitters." Now I knew why he was in such a poor mood for so long. I had seen the tracks on his arms but didn't see any withdrawal symptoms.

"Did Grub give you Heroin to help?"

"Yeah but your stuff is strong man too strong for me. I nearly overdosed the first night. Grub made your guys cut it down for me."

"How often do you inject now?"

"Twice a day but Grub is cutting it down every week. I have good days and bad days but Grub looks after me."

"So on the day of the accident you were drunk and high on Heroin?"

"That's why I couldn't stop man. I was done for if I'd stopped."

"So you managed to keep going. When you saw the papers the next day, did you see that a young guy had been charged with murder of the 5 passengers killed in the accident?"

"Yeah and I knew I had got away with it but the boss hit me around a fair bit. He got one of his guys to inject a heavy dose of Heroin into me and he nearly killed me but that dose was what made me Heroin dependant. From that day I had to get shot up; sometimes twice a day. After a few months twice a day was normal and sometimes 3 times a day. I was in a living hell. I wish I hadn't been released from prison."

"Were you sorry for the accident?"

"I'm sorry your friends were killed; I never wanted that, but I am not sorry you were framed for it as I didn't want to go back inside. I don't have a choice now; I'm here and you will make sure I get the heaviest sentence the law can give me."

"Why do you believe that Brown?"

"I ruined your life and killed your friends. You ended up here and got caught up in the prison gangs. You can't be happy defending me. You will find the best way to have me sentenced to the longest prison term you can get."

"That would give me the greatest pleasure Brown, but it ain't going to happen that way. I intend to make sure you get the best outcome for you and the State. If I can plea bargain I will. If I can find evidence that will get you released, I will use it. I will do what I have to do as a lawyer, to defend you with every breathe in my body, if only to show the world that the Aryan Brotherhood believes in Justice and fair mindedness."

"Won't that go against your creed?"

"The creed is to allow our Brotherhood to live with society not against it. Yes our aim in controlling the prisons of the USA is to push our creed, culture and lifestyle, but we are also aware that the prisons are full of others and many different colours and cultures. We have to live with that. You have been placed under our protection and we accept that. Having a black man in our midst is abhorrent to us but our creed is to protect what is ours, and quite frankly you are ours and might even become our first black Brother in time."

"Fuck man I don't want to become an Aryan Brother. What you going to do, bleach my skin?"

"Who says you can't become a Brother? If I tell my brothers you are willing to become a Brother then they will accept it. They do as I say."

"I know I'm going to end up in prison for the rest of my life. I have to be with my own kind. If you made me an Aryan Brother the tattoos you demand put on me would have me killed within minutes of me landing in a prison. Is that your plan of revenge?"

"Revenge? I don't have revenge on my mind right now, that's for later. Right now I have to defend you and I will need every ounce of your trust to do that."

Chapter 22

The pre-trial was due in 2 weeks and I was deep into the evidence I had uncovered. The Chief Prosecutor came to the prison along with the head of the PDO and I was summoned to the Warden's office. I was shackled while moved but the shackles removed outside of the Warden's office before I entered. I was introduced to both men by the

Warden as I had never met either man. The Chief prosecutor spoke first.

"Does he have to be shackled all the time Warden?"

"It is the prison policy for movement of gang members Sir."

"He is our representative here at San Quentin. Surely you can allow a more free movement for him?"

"We have rules here Mr. Prosecutor and I cannot have a rule for 1 and a rule for others."

"I understand. However, I am going to release Everett from his sentence pending a review of his case for a retrial. This means he is no longer a prisoner; however he will remain at your prison until released or resentenced."

"I don't want my sentence to be cut just yet. I need to be in control of the cellblock as leader of the Aryan's to maintain Brown's safety."

"I'm sure we can keep you locked up in H Block Everett." The warden said with a smile.

"I am releasing you under the care of the Warden. He is to be considered a private citizen Warden but in protective custody here at San Quentin. Do I make myself clear?"

"Yes Sir. I'm not sure how I can handle that but I will do my best to comply. I am still not happy with allowing him free access without shackles as he is a gang leader."

"I agree Warden, not an easy order for you. Mr. Everett will be considered a free man in your protection and will undergo a retrial immediately after the trial of Brown. I anticipate his immediate release after the trial. The evidence for a retrial is overwhelming. 3 people have been charged and sentenced over this affair and a 4th is yet to come to trial but that will happen within the next 2 weeks.

The trial of Brown will climax the investigation into his wrongful sentencing. From the evidence I have seen, Mr. Everett was wrongfully charged through corruption and not evidence. My sincere apologies Malcombe for what has happened to you in all respects. You have however, handled the briefs given to you well and I am sure we will have many a lively battle with you in court in the future. I wish you were on my side and not the PDO. You can always defect if you so wish? I would welcome you into my stable."

"I appreciate that Sir, but the PDO is where I believe I can do more good. I understand these kids better than anyone, and can help them. They are kids Sir, regardless of their crimes."

"We don't look at that Malcombe; we look at the crime and apply justice as we see the crime fits."

"I see the human side Sir and try to get a sentence that befits the man or the youth and not his crime. Many of these kids commit the crimes under duress or peer pressure. They are a result of their social standing in our wacked out social system. I'm sure that in time I will be banging on your door with plea bargains."

"I look forward to dealing with you Malcombe." The Warden then took the Prosecutor on a tour of the prison while I sat and talked with the head of the PDO.

"Sir, the freedom given to me this morning is not good. I need to be classed a prisoner regardless while I am here. I wouldn't know what to do with any freedom inside here. I know the rules and boundaries as a prisoner not as a free man in protective custody."

"I can't change what has happened but I will talk to the warden when he returns and if you like we can plead your case together."

"I'm sure he would welcome my remaining as a normal prisoner."

"Yes I'm sure he would." He did, and after our discussions I was taken back to Cell Block H and back to my own cell; and in shackles. It was my home and had been for 7 years. It was my little bit of sanctuary in a living hell. The shackles made me feel as I was part of the system again.

The day before the trial of Brown, we were both shackled; still dressed in our orange prisoner clothing and transported to the San Francisco Supreme Court, and placed in the cell block below the court. I had been asked previously if I wanted Brown and myself to be dressed in civilian clothing and had said yes and these clothes would be brought to us an hour before the start of the court. The jury still had to be picked and I needed to look as close to a lawyer as possible. I knew the tattoos on my face and hands would be clearly seen and the usual impressions made. Brown was unmarked facially but had several gang tattoos on his arms and body including his hands and knuckles; not as many as I had but enough that would have shown in the prison uniform had I decided they would be worn. Brown had to look like a young man with problems but not a murderer. I had managed to get the charges downgraded to Culpable Homicide which was 15 to 20 years each; Still a life sentence for him but the chance of parole in 50 years. Maybe I could get a 'Not Guilty' verdict if I played my cards right: But to get a "Not Guilty' verdict would then put my own release in jeopardy. Without a conviction, the PDO could not use this evidence in my retrial. I would then remain in prison for another 10 to 15 years. Could I handle another 10 to 15 years in prison? Yes. Therefore I had to go for a 'Not Guilty' verdict. I was his defence lawyer and I had to go for what I believed was right.

I met brown before the trial start. He looked good in the mid gray suit and pale blue shirt, open at the neck. I wore a dark charcoal suit with cream shirt and a red tie which felt like it was choking me. He laughed as I entered the interview room, and I also saw the funny side and laughed with him.

"The tattoos don't match the tie." He said laughing.

"The suit and shirt make you look good Brown. Your job is to tell the truth at all times when questioned, and make yourself look remorseful at all times."

"Yeah I know you told me before. You're going to try and get me off aren't you?"

"Yes, that's what a defence lawyer is for Brown. To try and get the client off."

"Why? If you get me off then you spend the rest of your life in jail."

"Would that be so bad? At least I get to help other kids like you get real help with the law. What do you think would happen to you with a normal lawyer?"

"Life maybe even Lethal injection."

"That's right so it's my job to get you off or at best the shortest possible sentence."

"I admire you Malcombe. As an Aryan Brother this must be the hardest thing you have ever done. You wanted to kill me didn't you?"

"Yes, but the Aryan brothers have long arms Brown so even if you get off this you are not safe. Your safest bet is to join us, black or not. We don't kill brothers unless we have to. I haven't ordered your death yet so be kind to me."

"You wouldn't let a black man join the Aryan brotherhood?"

"I might surprise you Brown, all you have to do is ask."

We were led upstairs to the court. Brown was handcuffed but I was free of all restraints. The judge entered and all stood. The charges were then read out and the judge asked us to plead. Brown stood up and answered loudly

"Not Guilty your Honour" and then we started the long and arduous task of picking the jury. I wanted mostly men, but mature mother figures were needed too. The men were working class not professionals. These men had to be able to relate to Brown and his life, the way he was brought up and the area where he lived. The women had to see Brown as their son so I had to appeal to the motherly instinct. It took us the rest of the day and an adjournment for lunch before I was satisfied of my choices of a jury. The prosecutor came over to me as we exited the court.

"I know what you're up to Everett. The boss told me to be careful of you."

"I enjoyed my conversation with him 2 weeks ago. A good man Kretzman and a fair one too. Don't underestimate me."

"You won't go for an acquittal; you have too much riding on this trial yourself."

"So you know my past do you? Well I assure you it is an acquittal I am going for, regardless of my own situation."

"Brave man Everett: How can you even consider trying to get an acquittal with what this man did to you?"

"It's because of what he did to me that I can help him. If he had not allowed me to be charged with the deaths of my friends, I would never have become part of the Aryan Brotherhood. I understand how these kids get entangled with the gangs out in the suburbs; become drug peddlers or drug addicts themselves. I understand how a man can kill another because he was told to do so. I understand the corruption of police and how it affects their lives every day. I understand these men far more than you ever will. That's why I can try for an acquittal with full confidence, regardless of the outcome for myself. I would rather do what I have to do and spend the rest of my life in jail than live with the knowledge I could have done more and didn't because it would affect my own life."

"I intend to go for the death sentence Malcombe, even though the charges are now 'Culpable Homicide'."

"I thought you would and will fight it hard. He doesn't deserve the death penalty. If he is found guilty I will fight for the smallest sentence and request 9 years for each count with parole after 5 years each."

"Why?"

'Because that's what I was sentenced to and he should be given no worse than I was. If I can get him off, you can still charge him with 'Dangerous Driving' and I will not defend him if you agree to a maximum of 1 year jail and 3 months non-parole. He will plead guilty to that offence and nothing more." He agreed and shook my hand.

"I will have him charged and sentenced immediately you know that?"

"I would expect that and he will too. He knows he has to go back to prison. How else could he become a member of the Aryan Brotherhood?"

"What, a black? You're pulling my leg Everett."

"Nope, he has asked to join us and I have agreed although he doesn't know it yet."

"Well that's a first."

"We all learn something new each day. The Aryan Brotherhood is against Blacks but we also have a creed and we defended this man for the last two years inside that prison. He has gained a lot of respect from my Brothers. Black or not he is the bravest man I know. The brotherhood respects that."

The prosecution started its statements and rambled on for most of the second morning. Brown sat passively and listened. The prosecutor made him out to be a gang thug; and drug addict and heavy drinker. He was an ex con who had evaded reporting to his parole officer on release so therefore technically was still a prisoner of the state. His entire background was pulled to pieces; his childhood and juvenile crimes; his serving sentences in Juvie and later in prison. He was shown by the prosecution to be an habitual criminal with no remorse and therefore had to be sentenced to prison for life if not to death.

I was asked to reply after the adjournment for lunch. I decided to stand directly in front of the jury so they could all see the tattoos on my face and hands. It was not to distress them but to show them I was of their social standing and no more. I answered every doubt the prosecutor had placed in their minds. I used his description of his childhood and prison sentencing as what was expected of a youth living in his area; how he had to join a gang to survive the streets, and I saw a couple of gentle nods; from both men and women. I decided that I would discuss the offences he was charged with in a broad sense.

"My client had been out of prison for just 4 days. He had been kidnapped and taken to a drug lord's base; the drug boss he had worked for as a teenager; injected with Heroin and sent out to the streets to deliver drugs. He bought alcohol to try and drown his sorrows as he didn't want to do what he was ordered to do, but the Heroin injected would make him dependant in the days and weeks to come. The alcohol mixed with the Heroin made his driving erratic and having not driven for 4 years he was unable to fully control the car. His car did hit the vehicle in question and 5 people were killed and1 seriously injured. Why did he run? Would you have stopped there waiting for the police when you were high on narcotics and possibly drunk? No, I doubt any of you would have. You would have run just like my client. With enough money, corrupt police can cover up your tracts but you might end up being beholding to some drug lord or gang leader. How do you get out of the clutches of a gang or drug syndicate? You can't and this was the situation with the defendant. A man was charged with the deaths of the occupants in the car. He was found guilty and sentenced to 70 years jail. So why has my client been charge for the same deaths? Why has the State decided two people were guilty? There weren't two guilty people, only one and he is already in prison serving his time. The evidence the prosecutor will present is the same evidence presented to the Public Defender's Office 10 years ago to convict or defend the person finally convicted of the "Manslaughter' of the 5 people in that accident. My client pleads not guilty of all charges because it has to be proved he was the driver of the car that originally hit the car whose occupants were killed. You as the jury have to decide without a shadow of a doubt that he was the driver and he killed those people. The slightest doubt in any of the evidence must bring a verdict of not guilty. That means on all 5 charges not just one or two; all five." I sat down and I saw brown was sobbing gently. "Why the sobs Brown?"

"You told them to leave you in jail. You said you had already been found guilty and therefore I couldn't be guilty. Why do that for a black man Everett?"

"You are not black; you are my client. I will use everything at my disposal to set you free, but you won't go free because the prosecutor has already told me you will be charged immediately if found not guilty with dangerous driving. I have agreed to a plea bargain of 12 months with a 3 month non-parole period with no objections to your parole regardless of what happened 10 years ago."

"Why the plea bargain?"

"You can't become an Aryan Brother outside of prison Brown."

"You honest; You will allow me to be a member?"

"I think the Brothers have already accepted you as a Brother Brown, you just have to be blooded in and tattooed. Oh don't forget we have to bleach you too."

"You got any bleaching soap?" We both laughed. We were both taken down stairs to the holding cells, Brown in cuffs and me free. I would not wear the cuffs or restraints while at the courthouse. After eating dinner I was allowed to join Brown in his cell on the pretext we had to plan the next day's strategy. To be honest, I needed my balls sucked dry. Brown was happy to oblige.

The prosecutor tried his best to lay blame for the accident on Browns shoulders but I had seen the video of the accident. Yes Brown had clipped the car but the intoxicated state of the car's occupants was more a contributing factor than Browns contact. I showed the video and explained the scene and how the car lost control because of the occupants' moving about unrestrained except one person. He sat in the middle of the back seat and you could see he was strapped into the seat. You could see how the occupants not strapped in swivelled and moved about, causing the car to swerve dangerously and then the impact with the wall and how the car started to break up and then collide with another wall on the far side of the freeway breaking in two and spewing out the inhabitants. Browns car was nowhere to be seen. Although Brown would have known he had clipped something, he would not know of the carnage left in his wake. I put enough doubt in the minds of the jury to give my case a hefty boost. The Prosecutor tried to counter the video but as it was the first time he had seen it, he was hard pressed to find anything to turn the jury around.

"It is clear members of the jury that the occupants of the car themselves were the major cause of the accident. The driver of the car seen to just barely clip the other car would not have realised the carnage he may have been involved with, especially if he had drugs or alcohol in his system. We must assume he had none as police had no chance to test the other driver within 24 hours of the accident. The person charged with the manslaughter of the 5 occupants was found to have a blood alcohol content of 0.207, 4 times the legal limit and would have surely cause him to be close to being comatose and therefore unable to have controlled the car when clipped from behind. I have another video for you to watch. This video is of similar accidents of vehicles hit in similar ways with the occupants of the vehicle hit in various stages of inebriation. The first is of a driver who is totally sober, the second of a driver just below the legal limit of 0.05, with drivers in subsequent accidents with reading showing up to 0.149. As you can see, as the alcohol content raises the control drops." The jury was fascinated and the prosecutor livid. The prosecution has to share their information with the defence but defence does not need to allow the prosecution the same benefit. Evidence and witnesses took 4 days and on the 5th day, which had taken us into the second week, we had to sum up. The prosecutor went first of course. He definitely went for the jugular saying the video evidence had tried to sway the jury away from the act of Brown's coming into contact with the car and causing the deaths. As Brown had left the scene it had become a charge of murder and with 5 charges, he would demand the death penalty as this was Browns' 3rd offence and therefore made him in the eyes of the law an habitual criminal. The State would demand the death penalty so the State did not have to feed, clothe and incarcerate Brown for the rest of his life which the State estimates to be around 60 years at a cost of $3 million dollars. His juvenile record once again was brought up as well as his prison record and his joining of gangs both inside and outside of prison. Brown was shown as a man ready to offend the instant he walked free.

I again walked close to the jury and looked them in the face. I again went over the whole scene but in the perspective of Brown and not how the prosecutor showed him. I tried to make Brown the victim; of his growing up and social situation. No father and a working single mum; were being left to his own devices well into the late night hours as his mother worked hard to put food on the table (working the mother side now on the homely looking women). I also emphasised his love for his mother and the evidence given by his mother as a called witness. How he sought to help his mother with money at an early age and how he got tangled with gangs and drugs. I asked the jury to look at where they themselves lived and ask themselves where their children would be tonight while they were locked inside a hotel room. Could their children become what Brown became? Would it be so hard for them to become gang members and end up in Juvie or prison? I went through the accident in clearer detail emphasising each point and finally I walked back to my desk.

"I don't believe you can find a verdict of guilty on any of the charges of murder. These charges have already been answered in a court of law and sentence given." I then walked over to the jury once again then looked at each member one by one. "Why do I believe you must give a verdict of Not Guilty?" Again I looked at each member of the jury. "You cannot find a man guilty of a charge that has already been sentenced when the State knows there was only one person involved. I was the person charged and sentenced for the manslaughter of those 5 people." There was a gasp from the court and from the jury. The judge called for order. The judge then instructed the jury as to each point from the prosecutor and the defence council. The jury eventually was led out of court to deliberate the case. We waited in a side room and food and coffee was brought to us. It was 3 hours before we were told the jury had reached a verdict. We all filed into the court once again and the jury brought in. The faces said nothing. The judge entered and we all stood.

"Members of the jury, have you come to a decision in this case?"

"Yes your Honour." The verdict was handed to the judge who read it and then passed it back.

"Leader of the jury, will you read the verdict. The defendant will rise and face the jury." Brown rose and faced the jury. The moment of truth was upon him and his face was showing strain.

"We the jury of 7 men and 5 women solemnly swear that this verdict is 100% unanimous and true. We find the defendant Not Guilty of all charges." Brown collapsed into his chair, tears streaming down his face utterly speechless. I just looked at him and smiled.

"Your Honour, with the acceptance of the defence, I wish to lay a charge of dangerous driving on his client."

"Mr. Everett, do you want this to proceed at this time?"

"Yes your honour and we will plead guilty."

"Very well, Mr. Prosecutor do you have a recommendation for me? I am sure you have already discussed this with the defence council?"

"Yes your Honour. We request your Honour consider a term of 1 year's jail with a non-parole sentence of 3 months. With time served we recommend the defendant be returned to prison and released within 7 days: His parole to be served in San Francisco and not LA."

"Mr. Everett?"

"We agree your Honour."

"So be it: Odawa Brown; you are sentenced to 12 months in the State Prison of San Quentin on the charge of dangerous driving causing injury for which you have pleaded guilty. You will serve a minimum period of 3 months before parole. With time served you are to be release immediately but within 7 days maximum to allow the necessary paperwork to be completed. This court is adjourned." We all stood and Brown looked at me.

"You sacrificed yourself for me. Why?"

"You are going to be blooded in and tattooed tonight my black Brother. I have work for you outside the prison walls."

"I don't want gang work running drugs and such."

"Who said it was running drugs? The Chapter also has legitimate business and we need men who can be part of the neighbourhood. We have a poor presence in a large black area of San Francisco and we have a betting shop there. It's legitimate so don't worry but I need some muscle to make sure there are no problems, but first we have to blood you in."

"I've got to kill someone haven't I?"

"Yes. My nemesis the leader of the Afro's: You will be protected and they won't know who did it. You will be tattooed but not where it can be easily seen and will require you to remove your shirt to be visible. What you have done later is your own decision."

"When is Grub due out of Prison?"

"He has about 6 months left. You really like him don't you."

"Yeah, I think I love him. He needs me to protect him."

We were returned to San Quentin prison and back to our old cells. That evening before lights out, Needles did his thing and then we made sure Brown was blooded in. We knew the leader of the Afro's used the showers about 30 minutes before lights out. Brown was waiting for him. He used his bare hands to snap his neck. He was blooded in. That night when he returned to the rec room before lights out, the Brothers gathered around him and hugged him. Snake was hesitant at first then followed suit with everyone else. He was found in the shower block after lights out, and the video showed nothing. Faber came to see me the next morning.

"Why Malcombe: Why destroy yourself to save a black man I know you hate?"

"Brown is as much a product of his environment as I am now. He deserved to be free Faber. I have been here 10 years and I kind of feel at home here. I can take it, he couldn't he would have been dead from an attack within days of joining the general population. The Afro's would never accept him after spending nearly 2 years in our cell block. He had to go free."

"Well I have some good news and bad news for you. What do you want first? "

"Start with the bad then cheer me up."

"I am aware you want to remain in prison and continue with the PDO. However, the State Governor has pardoned you and as of 1 hour ago you are a free man."

"Why a pardon?"

"You told a jury you had killed 5 people. You confessed in a court of law."

"No, I didn't confess; I said I was the man accused and found guilty of the deaths and was serving a prison term for that. The fact that I had pleaded guilty was of no significance in that trial."

"The fact that you got a not guilty verdict meant you could no longer receive a retrial. The governor was aware of the evidence that was corrupted against you and the sentencing of 3 people who tampered with evidence to get you convicted so he had to do something. A pardon was all he could do, so you will always be guilty of manslaughter Malcombe. Your prison record and convictions will always follow you."

"I expected that Faber although I didn't expect a pardon. Can I refuse the pardon?"

"No and I don't think the PDO want you too either. You will not require a parole officer although the parole office will monitor you in case you need help in any way. You will be given a small pension for 3 months to assist you to find work and housing then it stops. You will have an office in the PDO building but in a new section being set up. It will be for gang related crime and you will head it up. The other members of your team will all be ex prisoners like yourself and original gang members, so you won't look so out of place as their boss."

"What if I don't want that Faber?"

"I know you do Malcombe. You want to help these kids as best you can and your dedication was shown when you got Brown off even though it stopped your own retrial. You knew the consequences of your actions but you knew it was the best defence you could give him and you went for it. The prosecutor had nowhere to go with your defence and the chief Prosecutor was impressed and that's why he talked to the Governor. The retrial had already been agreed on but when things changed the Prosecutor then drew up the paperwork for a pardon and the Governor signed immediately. I watched you defence Malcombe and to be honest I would not have had the courage to have done what you did."

"So what is the good news?"

"Bonny will meet you outside the gate at 8am tomorrow morning. You will be given full access to San Quentin prison for future visits to inmates for their defence. Your criminal record will not hinder or impede your access by order of the Governor."

"Tomorrow morning at 8am you say?"

"Yes so prepare yourself."

"There are many I have to thank and farewell. That won't be easy."

"I know but you have a new life ahead of you Malcombe and your family wait for you. You have been through hell and back but you are a survivor. This new future will give you a life you could only dream about 10 years ago. Your wage will not be big Malcombe, barely subsistence level, but I don't think you ever expected that did you?"

"Bonny knows how to live well and cheap Faber. She has survived by herself for 10 years with 4 mouths to feed and support. I don't think a low wage will make any difference to her life."

Chapter 23

Faber brought Bonny out to the prison the next morning and dropped her off. She asked him to go and let them catch the bus back into town by themselves. It would give them time together. I was ready to move at 6 am but I was made to join the movement down to the dining hall for breakfast first before being called out, shackled and moved into the administration building. There I was unshackled, allowed a hot shower with soap that actually had a perfume and not the usual sour soapy wax smell and then allowed a decent shave. The barber was also there but he had a cut throat razor not his sheers. He shaved my head clean and smooth and I was then given clothing to dress with. A suit in beige; I threw away the jacket and wore only the pants: Brown shoes in a brogue style; cheap but ok. Underwear similar in quality to what we had to wear in prison, boxer style and cheap rough cotton. It was cold outside and I was offered a coat or a jacket. I chose the lightweight jacket. I wanted to feel the chill of the morning on me and the wind cutting through the cheap fabric. I was then escorted to the Warden's office for the customary 'goodbye see you again real soon' speech he gave to all prisoners on their release. But he didn't give me that speech.

"I admire what you did for Brown, Everett. I doubt any other lawyer in your situation would have done the same. To induct Brown into the Brotherhood was a neat trick. First time I ever saw that with the Aryan brotherhood." I smiled and he saw the smile. "You had a plan didn't you Everett;

you wouldn't have sworn in a black man into your Brotherhood unless there was a reason. Oh I know he killed Decker the other night as his 'Blood In' but I can't prove it so I'm not going to try. When does he take over the blacks in San Francisco Everett?"

"When you finish his paperwork Warden: You have a brilliant mind Sir but the prisoners are two steps ahead of you and always will be. It's the problem of prisons and prison management. You try to be one step ahead but in fact just lag behind. You can't stop the killings; you can't stop the drugs and you can't find all the weapons. All you do well is contain the social misfits of this world and even then some escape. Most prisoners don't need weapons to kill; most have powerful bodies that can snap a man's body in half with little trouble. No, weapons are for the week. You can search the Aryan's cell block and find nothing. The brothers are their own weapons."

"You tried to remain in prison didn't you. You cut any chance of a retrial by using that defence of Brown. Why do that for a black man when you are Aryan?"

"I had been in prison for the best part of my life. I had learnt to accept prison as my home. I am still an ex con Warden and a pardon does not exonerate me, merely allow me freedom. I didn't need freedom to be happy. I needed my Brothers to make me happy and the power they gave me. Balls will be the new leader inside of here from today and he does not have the logical sense I think I had. Expect trouble but don't expect to be able to solve it. He is as devious a man as I have ever met. Snake is the 2ic and a vicious man in all respects. No your troubles haven't begun yet Sir."

"Thanks for the warning."

"I believe I have been included on the visiting list of every Aryan brother in the prison. You will see me often Warden as their legal representative and I will be examining each and every trial of those brothers. If there is one small fact that should not have been used, I will ask for a retrial. Just imagine your prison without the Aryan Brotherhood? But of course that won't happen; we just can't stay out of trouble can we?"

"Guards, take him to the main gate and throw him out."

"Goodbye Warden; see you again soon but not in your care this time."

"I will keep a cell for you."

"My father is dead Warden and you yet have to answer to that crime and it is coming. Be warned Warden, you will be joining your wards before too long. I know my father colluded with you in LA and with the Warden of San Quentin." I walked out as two Federal Marshals walked in and arrested the Warden on corruption charges. The guards just looked at me and I smiled.

There was Bonny standing there in the hot sun and cold winds. She was alone as her mother had the children and would keep them for the night so we could have a night alone. She looked so good to me right then. She was dressed in a low priced dress in a heavy fabric and flat cheap shoes; she had on a top coat open at the front and her hands in the big side pockets. She smiled when she saw me but did not rush up and hug me. She waited for me to walk to her and our lips met for the first time since we had left each other the morning after our wedding. We always kissed on visiting days but could never kiss in a loving way. Today I kissed and hugged her as if I never wanted her to leave my arms. The bus arrived within seconds of my exiting and kissing Bonny. We boarded the bus and I paid the tickets with the $20 the prison had given me. We sat up the back and when we had sat down; I looked at her and smiled.

"You only got one person to visit in prison now and I am going to try and get him out."

Phillip Lesbirel

The Author - Skinphil

Skinphil is a Pseudonym used by Phillip Lesbirel. It is a name he uses for his new publishing company Gay Books Fetish and for books published from 2014 through this publishing company.

I have authored many books in many genre but am better known for my gay skinhead and skinhead books. I was born in Guernsey in the Channel Islands to a working class family and had a great family life and upbringing. Being from a working class family allowed me to see the world from a working class point of view and as skinheads are working class lads, I was able to relate to them. I always considered myself a skinhead and still have not hung up my boots. I was educated at the Guernsey Grammar School for Boys on a scholarship until 1965. I finished my GCE before immigrating with my family to Sydney Australia. After roaming the country for a few years I settled finally in Brisbane and Married, but after a serious car accident and 8 months hospitalization and rehabilitation, joined the Royal Australian Air Force as an adult Apprentice Motor Mechanic and Diesel Fitter and enjoyed 25 years of military service.

I retired from the military in 2002 and after living and working in an Indigenous Community in the Northern Territory and moving about once again, finally settled in Cairns in Far Northern Queensland in 2004. The climate suited me, being tropical and warm all year round. It was here that I started to write after I was divorced in 2005 and first published a novel in 2009, although my first completed novel was in 2006. That novel was 'A Trip to Hell' book 1.

Most of my books are of the gay genre and are listed at the back of this book. I have also published 4 books under general fiction to date and have found it rewarding to write none gay fiction. 'A Matter of Honour' is classed as a general fiction book although there are some sections that do show gay sex as part of the story line. '**Deep Sea Rig**' is my first attempt at a Science Fiction book. I hope you enjoy it as much as I did writing it.

A Ruined Life is about an 18 year old who wakes up in hospital after a serious car accident with multiple injuries, but finds himself in a prison ward. Later he is charged with Culpable Homicide on 5 counts. After a plea bargain, he is sentenced on 5 counts of Manslaughter and with other charges relating to the traffic act, receives a total of 70 years jail and a non-parole of 20 to 25 years. This book deals with his life in prison, his being forcibly made to join the Aryan brotherhood and his marriage to the leader of the Aryan Brotherhood's daughter.

Phil Lesbirel

Other books by this author under his real name of Phillip Lesbirel

General Fiction

The Diary of Errol Harbuckle – action thriller

The Blizzard – Two men trapped together and their interaction

The Swine Herder – an adult fairy tale

A Matter of Honour – skinhead honour

Deep Sea Rig – Science Fiction

Retribution - A skinhead story of love and its loss.

The Detective O'Neil Murder Mysteries - A mass murder and a prime suspect but did he really murder all 5 victims?

Gay Fiction

The Gay Mechanic – a gay love story

The Right to Live – gay youth suicide

Growth of Love – a gay love story

Hi, are you there – a gay love story with an occult twist

Life's Journey books 1, 2, 3, 4, 5 and complete story – A skinhead book

Daniel – skinhead book of love, vengeance and reprisals

Fighting Dog – skinhead white slavery and a search to find Ray

Diapers Stories book 1 – a compendium of short stories

Diaper Stories Book 2 – revised edition including a novelette

My life in diapers - Story of a boy who is forced into diapers and how he lives into youth and manhood in a diapered world.

A Collection of Short Stories, One Act Plays, and a Christmas Carol (plays are available for use by gay organizations copyright free, just let me know with an email of your intention to use. (philliplesbirel@gmail.com)

We Were Straight – two straight men, forming a bond then finding love

A Trip to Hell – Books 1, 2 & 3 and Trilogy complete and revised

My Life in Chains – Non consensual white slavery

My Choice, My Hell – A consensual paid prison stay turns to a real sentencing to the chain gang and finally Lethal Injection

Occult

The Devil's Seed – The Devil decides to wage war on the Christian world and spread his seed.

Hi, are you there - Love found in a most unusual way with spiritual and Occult undertones

Look out for new publications by this author over the coming months.

Printed in Great Britain
by Amazon